D0550154

THE BEGINNING . . .

"Stop being so mysterious," Douglas ordered. "Are you going into the prediction business?"

"Can you predict things?" Beth gasped.

I glanced her way. She looked absolutely awestruck. She was staring as if she'd never seen me before. Her mouth was slightly open and she seemed to be in unbearable suspense as she awaited my reply.

How impressed they'd all be, I thought, if I *could* predict things. They'd be hanging on my every word. No one would make a move without consulting me first. Being able to foretell the future was just about the most amazing talent anyone could have. Compared with that, piano playing, bowling, and acting were mere child's play. And as for scientific geniuses—well, not even a scientific genius would be able to figure out how to see into tomorrow. . . .

AND THIS IS LAURA

BY ELLEN CONFORD

AN ARCHWAY PAPERBACK
POCKET BOOKS . NEW YORK

POCKET BOOKS, a Simon & Schuster division of
GULF & WESTERN CORPORATION
1230 Avenue of the Americas, New York, N.Y. 10020

Copyright © 1977 by Ellen Conford

Published by arrangement with Little, Brown & Company.
Library of Congress Catalog Card Number: 76-53583

All rights reserved, including the right to reproduce
this book or portions thereof in any form whatsoever.
For information address Little, Brown & Company,
34 Beacon Street, Boston, Mass. 02106

ISBN: 0-671-29887-9

First Pocket Books printing April, 1978

Trademarks registered in the United States and other countries.

Printed in the U.S.A.

AND
THIS
IS
LAURA

1

I'll bet none of this would have happened if I hadn't been such an ordinary, run-of-the-mill person. If I'd been my sister, Jill, for instance, I'd have been too busy rehearsing *Romeo and Juliet* and winning bowling trophies; if I'd been my brother Douglas, my time would have been occupied with piano playing and captaining the Hillside High School debating team. Even my little brother, Dennis, is so busy memorizing TV commercials and doing his daily counting he hardly has time left for anything else.

Dennis is counting to a million. Why? I have no idea. Why do people climb mountains?

For a long time I was convinced I was adopted; how else could you explain the fact that while surrounded by a family of overachievers, there was absolutely nothing that I was brilliant at? Oh, I do well enough in school. Very well, in fact. Like almost straight "A's." But I don't do anything *special*. I mean, if my mother were introducing us she could say, "My daughter Jill, the actress. My son Douglas, the musician. My son Dennis; would you like to hear him do the Anacin commercial?"

But when she got around to me, what could she say? "And this is Laura. She's twelve."

Of course she wouldn't. She never has. She's a little casual about introductions anyway. She's a little casual about *everything*. What she usually says is "Meet the mob."

Nevertheless, being utterly average in my family is a tough row to hoe, believe me.

And it's not merely the lack of my outstanding ability that sets me apart. It is, in fact, a whole question of *life-style*.

Take breakfast, for instance.

Now, my idea of breakfast is: orange juice, scrambled eggs or cereal, toast and milk. A nice, normal, healthy breakfast, right?

For Dennis's breakfast, my mother plops fourteen different little packets of dry cereal on the table, each one of them coated with sugar, and lets Dennis eat whichever ones he wants. And he sits there wolfing down Sugar Stinkies and Cocoa Barfos and Hunny-Bunnies until I can practically hear his teeth disintegrating.

And when I point out that he's ruining his entire mouth with that junk, you know what she says? "He gets fluoride treatments."

Jill's breakfast consists of a stalk of celery, two tablespoons of wheat germ and black coffee. *Black coffee!* I mean, she's fifteen years old.

"Don't you realize she's going to stunt her growth with that?" I ask.

And my father says, "She's five foot six. How much growth can she stunt?"

Douglas eats frozen pizza for breakfast. That is, he doesn't eat it frozen—my mother sticks a couple of those packaged pizzas in the oven and heats them up. At least he has milk with them. My mother says pizza is a perfectly fine breakfast nutritionally because the cheese has protein and calcium and the dough is like toast or bread and the tomato sauce has Vitamin C, like orange juice. Okay. She's got me there. But it's not *normal.*

My father has been known to eat veal kidneys. He points out that in places like England kidneys are very commonly eaten at breakfast. But we are not living in England. We are living *here* and kidneys are *not* commonly eaten for breakfast in the United States. And the smell of kidneys cooking at seven o'clock in the morning . . .

Even Jill has threatened to report him to the Environmental Protection Agency for fouling up the air, but he just says, "Stop picking on my kidneys."

My mother doesn't eat breakfast. She drinks coffee. I don't blame her. Sometimes when I look

3

around at what the rest of the family is eating I lose my appetite too. But back in the first grade I learned that A Good Breakfast Is The Start Of A Good Day, so I force myself.

Now, this whole story has to begin somewhere (and it's about time, too) so since I've begun to fill you in on the hideous details of breakfast, we might as well start there.

It is a drizzly morning in late September as we look in on the Hoffman household. A typical Monday at 522 Woodbine Way, with nothing to distinguish it from any other Monday. As we join the Hoffmans, we hear Laura say . . .

"But that's not logical. If you're so concerned with our individual likes and dislikes at breakfast, how come we all have to eat the same thing for dinner?"

"Because preparing dinner is more trouble than preparing breakfast. Therefore, preparing six dinners would be six times more difficult than preparing five breakfasts."

"That's logical," my father said.

"And besides," my mother went on, "anyone who doesn't like what we have for dinner is always free to go and cook whatever he or she prefers."

"What's the matter, Joe? You're so grumpy today. Frankly, Bill, this irregularity is getting me down. I've tried everything—"

"Dennis, *please*. Not first thing in the morning." Jill held her hand to her head.

"Nagging headache? Why suffer? For fast, fast, fast relief—"

"DENNIS!"

"Douglas, dear, I think your pizza is burning."

He didn't look up from his newspaper. " 'S all right. I like it that way."

"It's not enough," I said irritably, "that he has to eat pizza for breakfast—it's got to be burnt pizza."

Douglas sighed and plopped his paper down on the table. "All right, all right, Fussbudget. I'll take it out so it doesn't offend your delicate sense of smell."

"Don't do it on my account," I snapped. "I was just worried about your being able to read the paper through all that black smoke."

"You're exaggerating slightly." He snatched the pizzas out of the oven and dropped them onto a plate. "As usual."

Douglas is sixteen. He's extremely sarcastic. I don't exaggerate. I report everything *exactly* as it happens.

"The first meeting of the dramatics club is this afternoon," I said, "so I'll be a little late."

No one was very impressed. Why should they be? Jill has had the lead in every play she's been in since elementary school. The last play I was in was a second grade production about the Basic Food Groups called something like "Mealtime Frolics of 1970." I played a grape. Along with thirteen other grapes I made up a bunch.

"You'll enjoy it," Jill said. "Is Mr. Kane still the advisor? He was really nice."

"Sure. He's my English teacher, remember? He asked me if I was going to join. He said, 'Your sister was so talented.' "

"He remembers me? Isn't that nice?"

That, I thought, depends on your point of view.

"What has that got to do with your joining the club?" my father asked.

I shrugged. "I don't know. I guess he thinks it runs in the family."

"Ridiculous," he scoffed. "You're an individual."

"And individual people," Dennis droned, "have individual hair problems. Don't settle for just any shampoo. Hi-Lite makes a shampoo that's just right for your particular hair problem. Cucumber for oily hair, strawberry creme for dry hair and Hi-Protein Egg for normal hair. Do you think my voice is getting any deeper?"

"Noticeably," my father said. Dennis is seven. He wants to be a TV announcer when he grows up.

Douglas folded up the paper and pushed his chair back. "Better get going. Coming, Bernhardt?"

Jill gulped down the last of her black coffee and jumped up.

" 'Bye, all."

" 'Bye, all," Douglas simpered and waggled his fingers at us. Jill whacked him on the shoulder.

6

I finished my eggs and cocoa and reminded Dennis that if he dawdled much longer he'd be late for school.

"Don't worry, Laura," my mother said, with a look of amusement. "I'll make sure he's not late."

"Okay, okay," I said hastily. "I was just trying to be helpful." Actually, I had very little faith in my mother's ability to get everyone's departure times straight. When she's working on a book, as she was then, she tends to become preoccupied with what's happening in her story and more than a little foggy about what's happening in the Real World.

My mother is a writer. Every day—or almost every day—after we've all gone to school and my father has left for work, she goes up to her room and writes for five hours. And then, four times a year, she sends a new book off to her publisher.

Two of the four are gothic romances. You know, with heroines who go to live in crumbling old castles where dark family secrets are buried and everyone acts strangely and the heroine finds herself in Terrible Danger. She writes those under the name of Fiona Westphall. The other two books are westerns.

Yes, westerns. With good guys and bad guys and gunfights—the whole bit. She writes those under the name of Luke Mantee. She picked that name in honor of Humphrey Bogart, who played a character named Duke Mantee in some movie.

Back before she was married and of course, before we all were born, my mother was in the movies. No one famous, you understand, just bit parts. Her movie name was Margo Lancaster. (Her real name was Maggie Luskin.) She certainly doesn't seem much influenced by the whole Hollywood experience. She doesn't even have a scrapbook, which I think is a shame. She says she never had anything to put in one.

I've read a few of her romances. They're pretty good, although they all seem very much alike. I asked her once wasn't it monotonous to keep doing practically the same book over and over again?

"Well, it's kind of a challenge," she said, "to write one story twenty-seven different ways, so that the reader never recognizes it's the same book."

The westerns I can't read at all. I think they're boring. Someone must like them though. My mother sells a lot of books. (She says the westerns are pretty much all the same too. But she seems to enjoy doing them.)

"Would you like a ride?" my father asked. "I'm just about ready to go."

"No thanks, I'll walk. I don't know why you have to go this early anyway," I added. "You could sleep late in the mornings, get up when you pleased—"

"But normal fathers don't do that," he teased. "Normal fathers get up at the same time every

8

day, have breakfast with their family, catch the same train to work—"

"Well it's no use pretending you're a normal father," I retorted, "so I don't know why you bother getting up early."

"Because I couldn't sleep through you kids in the morning; why fight it?"

Normal fathers. That's a laugh. Normal fathers are not, first of all, named Basil. (What *was* Grandma Hoffman thinking of?) Normal fathers are named Fred or Morris or George or David or Joe—no one's father is named Basil. And second of all, no one's father that I know has a laboratory all to himself at a huge corporation, where he's got no work to do at all but is just expected to fool around.

That's right, fool around. He doesn't have to *do* anything. He goes in when he wants to and comes home when he wants to and no one bothers him. It seems he's a scientist who was brilliant enough to be sought after by seven different companies who just wanted him to work in their lab (his own lab, really) because he might hit on something terrific which they could make a lot of money on. He also invents things. The company that finally got him pays him an enormous salary.

You wouldn't know it to look at him. He wears shorts and a Hawaiian print shirt in the summer (the same ones, every year) and gray work pants and a ratty looking gray sweatshirt in the winter.

And sneakers. When company comes he puts on socks. But he is, everyone says, a genius.

Now the question arises, wasn't I proud of him? And shouldn't I have been proud of my mother, the famous authors, and my sister, the actress and bowling champion, and my brother, the musician and captain of the debating team?

Of course I was. I thought they were all really amazing people. The thing was, I couldn't help wishing that a time would come when they would think *I* was amazing.

2

Junior High School is no big deal.

Back in the sixth grade they kept telling us how different things were going to be once we got into Junior High, and how we would be expected to act mature and be responsible and self-disciplined, but so far the only thing they were right about was when they told us there would be a lot more work.

The teachers keep saying we're supposed to act like young adults but they keep treating us as if we were still in sixth grade. We move around from class to class instead of staying in one teacher's room for most of the day, but then, in elementary school we went to different teachers for things like Art and Music and Gym and Library. The only big difference is that in Junior High you have hardly any time between classes, because they allow three minutes to get from one class to the next, and unless you have roller skates and a perfectly clear hallway, it is physically impossible to make it from one end of that building to the other in three minutes. And you couldn't roller-skate up two flights of stairs, anyway.

This particular day I was sitting in French class waiting for the teacher to arrive. The bell had rung already, and he was late. (I guess he forgot his roller skates.) It was the last class of the day and by the time I got to it I was pretty well up to *here* with school and feeling more like a caged panther than an enthusiastic learner.

As I sat there wishing for a bomb scare so they would have to clear us out of the school in no time flat and send us home, Beth Traub leaned over and asked, "Are you going to join the dramatics club?"

Beth was also in my English class, but I hardly knew her. We hadn't gone to the same elementary school. There are four elementary schools in our district but we all go to one junior high, which means that I didn't know about three-fourths of the kids in the seventh grade.

"Yeah, I guess I will." By this time the thought of staying in school an extra forty-five minutes, even for a club, didn't thrill me, but I had announced to everyone that morning that I was going to, so I felt sort of trapped.

"I am too," said Beth. "I'll meet you after homeroom, okay?"

"Okay. What room are you in?"

"108. What room are you in?"

"114."

"Wait for me, will you?"

"Sure."

Our teacher hurried into the classroom, panting slightly.

"*Bonjour, mes élèves.*"

"*Bonjour, Monsieur Krupkin.*"

"*Ouvrez vos livres à la page quatorze, s'il vous plaît.*"

He wrote "*p. 14*" on the board, because we were just beginning to learn numbers and hadn't gotten past *dix* (10) yet. Mr. Krupkin tried to speak only French in class and sometimes it got kind of confusing. After all, how much French could we understand after three weeks?

The period dragged by. We took turns reading aloud the parts of Pierre and Juliette, who go to *école supérieure* every day, where they *étudient* such subjects as *la géographie, l'histoire, l'anglais,* etc. After *école* they come home and have a glass of *lait* and some *petits gâteaux*. Then they do their *devoirs*. On Sundays they go for walks *dans le parc*.

It sounded like a very dull life.

I waited for Beth outside my homeroom. She got there a couple of minutes after the dismissal bell, staggering under a load of books, an instrument case and a gym suit half stuffed in a brown lunch bag.

"They ought to give us wheelbarrows," she grumbled, "along with lockers. I don't know how they expect us to carry all this stuff."

"Do you think they even *care?*"

"No. No, of course they don't care."

There were about thirty kids in Mr. Kane's room when we got there. Twenty-eight of them were girls.

Mr. Kane surveyed the group and smiled.

"Welcome to the Hillside Junior High School Drama Club," he said. "I'm delighted to see so many budding young thespians with us. I'm sure we're all going to have a lot of fun in this club as we learn some of the rudiments of acting. For those of you who are new to the club I want to tell you that we put on two plays a year so you'll have a good opportunity to develop your talent in front of live audiences. What I thought we'd do today is a little improvisational pantomime. Pantomime is acting without words; you use movement and action to convey what you're doing or feeling to the audience. We'll do simple, everyday things you've done all your lives, but you'll use no props, no words, just your imagination. Who wants to start?"

There was some foot shuffling and a few nervous titters, but no one volunteered. We certainly were a shy group, considering that we should have been eager to get up in front of an audience and act our hearts out.

Finally Mr. Kane said, "Why don't we have one

14

of our old members start off, so you'll have an idea of what I'm talking about? Jean, would you? And let's introduce ourselves as we perform."

A plump, very pretty girl with light brown hair walked to the front of the room. She didn't look nervous at all. She looked perfectly at ease in front of twenty-nine pairs of eyes.

"I'm Jean Freeman," she announced.

"Jean played the lead in *Sweet Sixteen* last year," Mr. Kane said. "Jean, why don't you do brushing your teeth?"

She nodded.

Facing us, she took an imaginary toothbrush out of its holder and stuck it in her mouth. She held it there, her mouth slightly open, while she picked up an invisible tube of toothpaste and twisted off the cap with two fingers. She took the brush out of her mouth and squeezed toothpaste on it. Then she put the tube down on the side of the "sink" and reached for the water faucet.

It was amazing. Her movements were so realistic you could almost see the water running and the toothbrush in her hand. She put the brush under the water a couple of times and even examined her teeth in the mirror above the sink as she brushed them. She rinsed off the brush and stuck it back in the holder, then turned off the water. She peered into the "mirror," baring her upper lip and running her tongue over her teeth. She even picked at the spaces between two teeth with her fingernail, as if she'd missed something. Then she

15

gave a little satisfied nod of her head, capped the toothpaste and put it back on the side of the sink.

"That's it," she said, and broke the silence.

Everyone burst into applause.

Jean walked back to her seat and Beth whispered, "Isn't that something? I could almost hear the brushing noise."

"Me too. She's really good."

"Thank you, Jean," said Mr. Kane. "Now that you have an idea of what you can do with pantomime, who else would like to try?"

Jean must have inspired us. This time quite a few people waved their hands to be called on, and even I felt the urge to try a pantomime. It looked like fun.

The next person was a short girl with dark, curly hair.

"I'm Rita Lovett," she said, almost in a squeak.

Mr. Kane had her put on shoes and socks. She wasn't nearly as good as Jean Freeman had been. In fact, if I didn't know she was supposed to be putting on shoes and socks, I would have thought she was tromping on ants and spraining her ankles because all she really did was raise and lower her feet a couple of times and kind of hold her hands on them.

Beth looked at me and shrugged, ever so slightly, as if to say, "Either one of us could do better than that."

I nodded to show I agreed.

16

"That's not bad, Rita," Mr. Kane said. "But remember when you do pantomime there are lots of little details that make it realistic and if you leave them out it's not as effective. Can anyone suggest something that Rita might have done even before she started to put on her socks?"

What was she supposed to have done *before* putting the socks on? I couldn't imagine. It seemed to me that Rita's problem was mainly that when she was supposed to look like she was putting on socks she actually looked like she was stomping on bugs, but apparently that wasn't what bothered Mr. Kane.

"She should have gotten the socks from the drawer," said Jean from the back of the room. "And then she should have unfolded them, or unrolled them or something like that."

"Right. You remember, Jean didn't start right off brushing her teeth. She did all the preliminary things you do first, uncapping the toothpaste, turning on the water. It's those little details that help your audience really see the thing you're acting out."

Beth and I both raised our hands. He called on me.

I went to the front of the room and looked back at all those faces. Beth smiled encouragingly at me. I tried not to show that I was nervous.

"I'm Laura Hoffman."

"Laura's sister, Jill," Mr. Kane said, "was in

this club a few years ago. She had exceptional talent. It seems to run in the family."

I sighed. I wished Mr. Kane wouldn't make such snap judgments. After all he hadn't even seen me act yet and now that he had everyone expecting I'd be as good as my incredibly talented sister, I felt more self-conscious than ever.

Everyone waited for me to do something terrific.

"Make a peanut butter sandwich," Mr. Kane said.

Peanut butter sandwich. Why, I'd done that hundreds of times. I reached for a jar of peanut butter above my head, like I was getting it from a kitchen cabinet. But I couldn't really *feel* it in my hand. How big was the jar? How wide did my fingers spread when I held a real jar of peanut butter?

I got the bread and put it down next to the peanut butter. I held it in two hands, although I was pretty sure that wasn't the way I usually carried bread around. Again, with the knife, I couldn't "feel" how I would ordinarily hold a knife. Did I just clutch it, or did my index finger extend over the handle?

I stuck the knife into the peanut butter jar and pulled it straight out. I think I did the spreading part pretty well, like I was really smearing on peanut butter. But apart from that, I knew I wasn't much good.

It felt so strange. I mean, even though all those people were watching me, what bothered me most was that I couldn't remember how it felt to hold a jar or a knife, things I did every day. It was mystifying that a peanut butter sandwich was so much more complicated to make in pantomime than it was in real life.

"Not bad, Laura." Was it my imagination, or did he actually sound disappointed?

A little let down, I went back to my seat.

"Did anyone notice anything Laura forgot to do when she made her sandwich?"

Rita Lovett waved her hand. Without waiting to be called on she blurted, "She forgot to take the lid off the jar!"

She smiled triumphantly, as if she'd somehow made up for not unrolling her socks by noticing my jar lid.

Beth looked disgusted. "She just couldn't wait," she whispered, "to pick on someone else's tiny mistake. I thought you were very good."

I was grateful for her sympathy. But I was so annoyed with myself! How could I forget a dumb thing like the jar lid, when I'd been so careful to look out for just those little details Mr. Kane warned us about? I remembered to put stuff back in the cabinet—I even put the knife in the sink, although probably no one knew what I was doing. I guess I'd been so busy looking out for all the little details that I forgot to watch out for the big ones.

Beth was next. She had to make a telephone call. Without talking aloud, of course.

She was good. She moved her lips and made faces and reacted like she was really having a conversation with someone. You could even see her leaning against a wall that wasn't there and fiddling with the curly telephone cord.

I made little clapping motions as she came back to the seat, and she grinned.

No one could find anything wrong with her pantomime.

"That's all we have time for today," Mr. Kane said. There were a few groans of disappointment from some of the people who still had their hands up.

"We'll do some more next week," he promised. "And I'll have some monologues prepared for you to read too. And after that, we'll begin to talk about our first play of the season."

The room buzzed with excitement. A lot of the shyness had apparently been overcome.

"And maybe," Mr. Kane went on, "you boys could get some of your friends to come down and join us. We'll need some male actors for our productions, you know."

The boys didn't say anything. They looked slightly uncomfortable. They hadn't done any pantomimes or even raised their hands during the whole meeting. I wondered if they'd stumbled into the wrong room by mistake and had been too embarrassed to just get up and walk out. One of them looked really young, like a fifth grader, and the other was tall and skinny with stuck-out ears. Neither of them looked like a potential leading man.

"You were so good," I told Beth as we walked out of the building.

"Oh, it's just that he gave me such an easy one to do. Yours was much harder than mine. Try it, you'll see how simple it is."

"I will when I get home." In fact, that's just what I'd been planning to do. She'd made it look like fun to make an imaginary telephone call and I couldn't wait to try it in front of a mirror.

Beth and I certainly seemed to be on the same wavelength. Though I hardly knew her, I did know right away that I liked her and wanted to get to know her better.

"Where do you live?" she asked. "Do you get the bus?"

"No, I walk. You know where Woodbine Way is?"

Beth shook her head.

"In Old Hillside Gardens."

"Oh, sure, I know where that is." She nodded.

Old Hillside Gardens is an area of Hillside with big, old houses, no sidewalks and lots of tall trees and broad lawns. They call it Old because right near it they built New Hillside Gardens, which has big modern houses, smaller, younger trees and sidewalks.

"We're in Country Manor," Beth said. "I have to get the late bus."

Country Manor is a lot like New Hillside Gardens but newer and way over on the other side of town.

"Hey, why don't you come home with me?" she said. "They don't care who gets on the late bus. They don't even check the bus passes."

I hesitated. I wanted to, but it was already late and I had so much homework to do and I didn't know how I was going to get home.

"Come on," she urged, starting to walk toward the waiting bus. "We can do our homework together, and my mother could drive you home. Or you could stay and have dinner with us."

"Well . . ."

"Come on, we'll miss the bus."

"Well, if you're sure your mother wouldn't mind—"

"Of course she wouldn't mind. She's always telling me to bring my friends home."

Beth already thought of me as her friend. I liked that.

"And if we get our homework done fast," she went on, "we can think up pantomimes for each other to do."

"Or," I said, following her on to the bus, "we could do one the other person has to guess. To see how realistic we can be."

"That's a good idea. Like charades."

The bus pulled away just as we got into seats.

"Oh," I said suddenly.

"What?"

"I guess I accept your invitation."

Beth laughed.

3

The first thing I noticed about Beth's house was how quiet it was. No one was pounding on a grand piano. No one was rehearsing the role of a madwoman in the dining room. No one was raving about the impact of Ultra Brite on his love life.

True, there was the sound of Fred and Wilma Flintstone arguing in another room, but it was not simultaneously combined with all of the above, as it is in our house.

The second thing I noticed was how neat and orderly everything was. There was no clutter in the living room; a big bowl of fresh fruit was the only thing that sat on the glossy surface of the dining room table. In our house, if you want to eat in the dining room it's a major production.

You practically have to hire a bulldozer to clear away the debris.

I waited for Beth to tell me I had to take off my shoes to walk across the pearl gray wall-to-wall carpeting, which looked brand new. I had been in houses where that was required, but Beth just led me through the living room and dining room to the kitchen without a word about keeping the rugs clean.

Beth's mother was having a cup of coffee at the kitchen counter when we came in. The counter was in the center of the kitchen and divided it in half. Like everything else in the room, it gleamed.

"Hi, honey." Mrs. Traub put down her coffee cup and looked up from the newspaper.

"Hi. Mom, this is Laura Hoffman. She's in the dramatic club too."

"Hi, Laura. How did the meeting go?"

"It was fun," Beth said. "Is there anything to eat?"

She rummaged through the copper-colored refrigerator and came up with Hawaiian Punch, chive cheese and two pears. Then she took a box of crackers and a bag of potato chips from a cabinet.

"Leave some room for dinner," Mrs. Traub said mildly.

"We will." Beth lined up everything on a red enamel tray, along with glasses and knives. "Listen, is it all right if Laura stays for dinner?"

"No, really, I can't." I didn't want to just barge

in like that and have Mrs. Traub worrying about how to stretch the lamb chops to feed an extra mouth.

"Of course you can," Mrs. Traub said. She didn't seem to be counting lamb chops in her head. "It's only going to be spaghetti and meatballs, Laura, and I've got plenty. We'd love to have you."

"Well—if you're sure it wouldn't be too much trouble." I did want to stay. I felt very comfortable in Beth' shouse.

"It isn't *any* trouble. It's all made already, except for the spaghetti; we just have to put an extra plate on the table, and if it makes you feel better, I'll let *you* do that."

She grinned at me, and I smiled back. She was very pretty, younger than my mother and a lot more dignified looking. She had on this cream-colored pantsuit with a brown and beige striped sweater. My mother, who could be absolutely stunning if she felt like it, is about as clothes-conscious as my father. She's partial to old jeans and sweat shirts with pictures of Beethoven on them. When she goes out shopping, she throws a fringed shawl over this outfit. She has even been known to rush out for a carton of milk in the winter with a twenty-year-old mink coat draped over her sweat shirt and jeans.

If I protest that people will think her even more eccentric than they already do, she replies,

"But it's coming back in style. This type of coat is just what they're wearing now."

Beth's mother was waiting for my response.

"Come on, Laura," Beth urged. "Stay."

"Okay," I said. "Thank you. I'd better call home and tell them."

I followed Beth upstairs. The sound of the television was barely audible up there and in her room, with the door closed, you couldn't hear it at all.

"You can use the phone in my parents' room," Beth said. "Just shut the door so you can hear yourself talk. My brother sits in front of that TV all afternoon."

"How old is he?"

"Seven. He's a real brat."

"So's my brother. Seven, I mean."

"We ought to get them together," Beth said. "At *your* house," she added quickly.

After I called home we ate the cheese and crackers and pears. Beth's room was as neat and quietly elegant as the rest of the house. Everything was white and yellow and green; it would be summer all year round in there.

"Your mother's nice," I said as we finished off the potato chips and juice.

"Yeah. You'll like my father too. They're okay. You won't like Roger. But that's all right. Nobody likes Roger, except my parents."

"You have a great house," I said enviously.

28

"Wait till you see mine. It looks like a rummage sale."

I began to wonder what Beth would think of my family when she saw the way we lived. It's not that we would be condemned by the Board of Health or anything. It's just that the place always looks like a crazed litterbug has just run amok through it. My mother has a woman who comes in to clean every Friday and before she comes we dash around trying to put away the clutter that's amassed during the week so she can get to things like floors, countertops, etc., but within a day or two all the stuff somehow reappears in the living room and dining room and you'd never know that underneath all that mess it was really clean.

"We have a maid come in Mondays, Wednesdays and Fridays," Beth said. "It would never look like this if she didn't. My mother's a lawyer."

Well, that explained why she was all dressed up. After all, even my mother wouldn't go out to work in a sweatshirt and jeans. Although my father does, come to think of it. . . .

We had planned to do our homework, but every time we picked up a pen and actually started to work one of us would begin talking and we'd forget what we were supposed to be doing. We found we liked the same books, watched the same TV programs and hated the same things in school —graphs, maps and fractions.

We agreed that Jean Freeman would probably be the star of any play Mr. Kane's club put on.

We were just about to give up on the homework and do pantomimes instead when Mrs.
Traub called us to set the table.

I followed Beth as she bounced down the stairs
and was suddenly aware of how at home I felt
here. I could very easily get used to living surrounded by quiet elegance, I thought. It was quite
a comfortable feeling.

Since Beth knew where everything was, she
carried in all the dishes and forks and things and
I set the table. We *do* set the table at my house, in
spite of what you might think. As a matter of fact,
we use a very old, fancy set of china that my
Grandmother Hoffman gave us. It's practically an
heirloom. We also use real silver and cloth napkins. My mother says she likes to set a nice table.
It never seems to bother her that we usually eat in
the kitchen, and that it might strike people as a
little silly to use all that good stuff when stacks of
pots and half-empty packages of macaroni and
little heaps of recipes and clippings surround you
on all sides and you know you're eating in the
midst of this mess because you can't get into the
dining room. . . . But as long as the *table* looks
nice she doesn't care.

Beth's mother had changed her clothes. She was
now wearing plaid slacks and a turtleneck
sweater. She didn't look one bit less classy than
she had before.

"This is my father," Beth said. "Daddy, this is
Laura Hoffman."

"Hello, Laura." He turned to his wife. "Isn't it amazing, Lee? The older Beth gets the prettier her friends get."

Mrs. Traub just smiled, like she had heard that before.

I, on the other hand, hadn't. At least, not from a father who looked like *him*. He was *much* younger than my father and he could have been a male model. He had dark blond hair, dark brown eyes and had either just come back from Miami Beach, or used Insta-Tan.

I realized I was staring. I quickly went back to setting the table.

"Did you call your parents, Laura?" asked Beth's mother.

"Yes, I did before."

"That's good. Beth, get Roger away from the television, please, and tell him we're eating."

Beth sighed. "All right. Where'd you leave the leash?"

I giggled. She went into the living room and yelled, "ROGER! COME AND EAT!"

"If I wanted someone to scream for him, I could have done that myself," Mrs. Traub pointed out.

I couldn't believe she'd ever scream about anything.

Beth disappeared from the living room and came back a few moments later propelling her brother by a firm grip on the back of his neck.

31

"You don't have to choke me to death," the boy whined.

"Laura, this is Roger."

"So," I said, smiling at him. "The famous Roger."

"Who said I was famous?" he demanded.

"I just meant—well, Beth told me a lot about you."

"Beth's a liar."

She gave me a look of disgust and shrugged her shoulders.

Roger spent most of the meal twirling incredible amounts of spaghetti onto his fork and insisting everyone watch while he forced them into his mouth.

"Bet you think I can't eat *this* one," he'd say, and cram it in.

"How gross," Beth declared. She turned away.

I didn't watch him after the first time. It was much pleasanter to keep my eyes on Beth's father.

He ate very nicely.

Apart from Roger the meal was fine. Mr. and Mrs. Traub made me feel right at home and the food was very good. Beth and I told them all about the classes we had together and the drama club meeting.

They seemed interested in whatever we had to say and didn't ask dumb questions like "What do you want to be when you grow up?" or "So, how does it feel to be in Junior High School?"

We had apple pie and ice cream for dessert and

before I knew it, Beth and I had loaded the dishwasher and it was time for me to go home.

"I'll drive you," Mr. Traub offered.

"Oh, no, that's all right. My mother or father can come pick me up."

"Don't be silly," he insisted. He put his jacket on and walked toward the door.

"I'll go with you," Beth said. "Come on, your books and things are upstairs."

"Well, okay, thank you." I turned to Mrs. Traub "Thank you for dinner and everything. I really enjoyed it."

"You're welcome, Laura. You come again now, anytime. It was fun having you."

I got my books and jacket from Beth's room. She grabbed her sweater off the bed and we went downstairs.

"Goodby, Roger," I called to him. A burst of gunfire exploded in another room, so I didn't really expect him to hear me. But just as we were going out the door there was a faint, " 'Bye," from somewhere inside the house.

I gave Mr. Traub directions to Woodbine Way and when we pulled up in front of the house I told Beth, "You'll have to come to my house next time." But my heart wasn't in it. I said it because I thought I ought to, but what I really hoped was that Beth would keep inviting me to *her* house. What in the world would she think of my family and the way we lived, compared to her surroundings?

If I could just stall for time; I liked Beth and I expected we'd be good friends, but I would have liked to be absolutely secure about that before I brought her home with me to meet "the Mob."

"It didn't look like I'd have much time to stall with. The moment I issued my polite invitation, Beth said, "Great! When?"

4

"Well, here we are," I said nervously as Beth followed me into my house the next week.

"What a terrific place," Beth marveled. "It's just beautiful."

"Don't jump to conclusions," I warned her. "Wait till you see the rest of it."

"Anybody home?" I practically whispered, hoping that no one would hear me. That way I could lead Beth right up to my room, which was a relative oasis of neatness and quiet.

"In the kitchen," my mother called. She has ears like a bat.

". . . suppose a stiletto would be better than a dagger?" she was saying as I brought Beth into the kitchen. "I can never remember which one is long and thin."

My father, dressed in his usual depth-of-fashion style, was leaning against the refrigerator juggling three eggs—something he does when he's trying to figure out some knotty work problem that's hanging him up. My mother was in a chair, tilting it back on two legs and defying gravity to toss her over on her head.

"Oh, hi!" she said. She brought the chair forward with a thunk. "You must be Beth."

"Pleased to meet you," said Beth.

My father caught the eggs neatly in one hand and reached his other hand out for Beth to shake.

"Hello."

"Hello," Beth said. "You're really a good juggler."

"Thank you. But they're hard-boiled," he added modestly.

"Even so . . ."

"Well, it's just a hobby."

"Do you girls know whether it's a dagger or a stiletto that's long and thin?"

"Gee, I don't know," I said. I cast a sideways glance at Beth. She looked a little confused. "Why don't you look it up in the dictionary?"

"That's a very good idea," my mother agreed, "except that I can't find the dictionary. You see, I want Linnet to see the blade glinting in the moonlight, and if the swarthy stranger has it pressed against her throat, I'm not sure that enough of the blade would extend out past her chin so that she could see it."

36

"Why don't you make it a saber?" my father suggested. "That's plenty long enough." He resumed his juggling.

"Oh, no," my mother said impatiently. "You can't carry a saber around in your teeth. Besides, this creep would never slink through back alleys shlepping a saber."

"She's writing a book," I hastened to explain before Beth ran screaming from the room. To be perfectly honest, Beth didn't seem to be ready to run at all. In fact she appeared utterly fascinated by the whole ridiculous conversation.

"Writing a book! How marvelous! What's the name of it?"

"I'm not sure. Either *The Dark Side of Eden* or *Shadows in Paradise*. Which do you like better?"

"They're both wonderful titles. I don't know how you can pick."

"Maybe a dirk," my mother said suddenly. "Does anyone have the *remotest* idea of what a dirk looks like?"

"Come on, Beth. Let's get something to eat and go up to my room." But Beth wasn't in much of a hurry to escape from my parents.

"What kind of a book is it? Have you written anything else?"

"Oh, lots," my mother told her. "This one is a gothic romance. You know, where the heroine marries a mysterious stranger she hardly knows and goes to live in the old family mansion—"

"Oh yeah, I've read some of those. Maybe I've

even read something you wrote without knowing it."

"Come on, Beth. Let's go upstairs."

"What are some of the names?" she persisted.

"Let's see, there's *The Secret of Cliffhaven, The Second Mrs. Marlowe, Legacy of Fear, The Crompton Estate, The Diary of Lydia Blake*—"

"You wrote all *those?*"

"She wrote more than that," I answered irritably. "Come on, Beth, we were going to practice our monologues."

"In a minute, in a minute. You know, the minute I get home I'm going to the library and look for some of your books."

"You probably won't find too many of them in the library. They're all paperbacks. But we've got lots of them around. Why don't you borrow some if you feel like it?" My mother looked over at me, standing with my arms folded across my chest and my lips tightened into a narrow line.

"Guess I'd better get back to work," she said. She stretched lazily and uncoiled herself from the chair. "You're staying for dinner, aren't you, Beth?"

"Yes, thank you."

"See you later."

"Excuse me," I said pointedly to my father, who was blocking the refrigerator. He moved to the sink without ever stopping his juggling. Beth just stared.

I was collecting Cokes and a big bag of popcorn when Dennis came wandering in.

"Do you think I could count to afinity?" he asked my father.

"You mean *in*finity?"

"Yeah, that's what I mean."

"No, I don't think so."

"Why not?" Dennis asked.

"Because you'd never get there."

"Why not?"

"Because that's what infinity means."

"Oh." He sounded disappointed. "Well, I don't know what I'm going to do after I get to a million."

"You could count to two million," my father suggested.

"No, that would just be the same thing. I wanted to do something different."

I had to practically drag Beth out of the kitchen.

"He's so cute," she said. "Not at all like Roger. And so *smart*."

"Yeah," I agreed sourly.

We were no sooner up in my room with the door shut than Beth remembered she wanted some of my mother's books. I had been marveling at how fortunate it was that Jill and Douglas were out and I was looking forward to a nice, quiet afternoon of rehearsing our monologues. But Beth insisted that she had to get the books *now*, or she'd forget.

Back downstairs to the den. Beth exclaimed over the two shelves of my mother's books.

"But what's this?" She pulled out one titled *The Last Trail*. "Why is this in here? Who's Luke Mantee?"

"My mother," I sighed.

"Your *mother?* You mean she wrote this too?"

"And this one, and that one, and this one—" I yanked them off the shelves and practically hurled them at her. *Showdown at Coyote Pass, The Longest Ride, Laramie's Way* . . .

"Can I borrow these too?"

"Do you like that stuff?"

"I don't know; I never read any of it. But just knowing your mother wrote them—you must really be proud of her."

"I guess so."

Beth looked curiously at me. It was probably the first time she'd looked at me at all since we'd gotten home.

"Is something wrong?"

"No, nothing's wrong."

"Are you mad at me?" Beth asked. "Did I say something—"

"No, I'm not mad at you." But I sounded as if I was. "Really," I added gently, "really, I'm not."

Beth carried an immense pile of my mother's books upstairs and put them on top of her looseleaf. I assured her that we had plenty of copies and it was all right to take that many home with her.

40

Finally we settled down to our monologues.

Beth read hers very well, even though Mr. Kane had just given them out that afternoon. It was a funny one and Beth has a natural flair for comedy. I sipped my Coke and listened and when she was finished I applauded.

"That was terrific," I said. "You were as good as Jean Freeman." Jean had read the same monologue in front of the club.

"Oh, I was not."

"You *were*. You're every bit as good as she is. I just hope Mr. Kane isn't so blinded by her past successes that he automatically makes her the star of everything."

"Oh, come on." She refused to believe me. But it was true. She was good.

I had a dramatic monologue. Maybe I would have done better with comedy, but on the other hand, my mind wasn't on acting at all, so perhaps it wouldn't have made any difference. I kept thinking, wait till she meets Jill. After all she's heard about her from Mr. Kane—and wait till she hears Douglas play the piano. Beth was in the school orchestra; she played the flute, and she was sure to think Douglas's original composition for piano were brilliant, not to mention his playing. . . .

She'd end up feeling sorry for me. She'd wonder how a family like mine could have produced such a talentless, un-outstanding member. Why, compared to my mother or father, compared to Jill and Douglas—even compared to Dennis, I was *boring*. There was absolutely nothing special about me in any way. It wouldn't take long for Beth to realize that, and then—

Well, of course the more I thought about this the less I could concentrate on acting and the worse my reading became. Just as I was nearing the end, the sound of a piano shattered the unaccustomed calm.

"Ohh!" I growled and tossed the mimeographed sheet aside. "What's the use?"

"You were doing fine," Beth said loyally. "You just got distracted by the piano. Who's that playing?"

"Douglas. I told you about him."

"Oh yeah. Is that one of his own pieces he's playing?"

"I think so. I can't really tell."

"Open the door, okay? I'd like to hear him."

I could hear him just fine with the door closed. A grand piano has the kind of sound that can fill a whole house. And as far as I know, Douglas has never composed anything soft. But then, I'm not a musician, so perhaps that makes a difference. I opened the door.

"Hey, that's pretty tricky," Beth commented. "Could we go and listen to him for a while? Do you think he'd mind?"

"Oh, no," I sighed. *"He* wouldn't mind at all."

As a matter of fact he didn't even hear us clatter down the stairs and into the living room.

He didn't know we were around at all until he finished playing the piece, when Beth jumped up from the sofa and ran over to the piano.

"Oh, that was super!" she cried. "Did you really compose that?"

Douglas didn't seem to be surprised either at the praise, or the stranger standing next to the piano.

"Yeah. You like it?"

"I love it. Would you play it again? From the beginning? We were upstairs and I didn't hear the whole thing."

Drowned out by my monologue, no doubt. I sighed and sat back on the couch, resigned to hearing the whole thing again.

"What's it called?" Beth asked. "It sounds sort of ragtimish."

"It is. It's called 'Intensity Rag.' It's kind of a combination of ragtime and classical. It's my own invention. I'm trying to think up a new classification for it."

"You mean like jazz, or classical or something?"

"Yeah, right."

"How about," Beth giggled, " 'Classtime'?"

Douglas laughed. He looked over toward the couch where I was patiently waiting for the encore to begin and end. "Hey, don't you introduce people to your family?"

"Beth, this is my brother Douglas. Douglas,

this is my friend, Beth. Consider yourself introduced."

"Have you composed anything else?" asked Beth.

"Oh, sure, lots of things." He shrugged.

I was beginning to get a feeling of déjà vu. Hadn't she just had this same conversation with my mother not an hour ago?

"Isn't that terrific? I play the flute," she said shyly "but I'm really nothing much."

"She's in the school orchestra," I said. I'd had it with Beth's modesty.

"Well, you have to start somewhere," Douglas said. He sounded unbearably smug. You certainly won't hear any false modesty from Douglas. Come to think of it, you hear precious little *true* modesty from Douglas.

"I'll never be as good as you are. I couldn't even *dream* of composing anything."

Douglas practically purred.

"You ought to," he said to me, "bring your friends home more often."

Looking pleased at this roundabout flattery, Beth floated back to the couch. She folded her hands carefully in her lap, fixed her gaze on Douglas's magic fingers and exhaled.

"Play it again, Douglas."

He bowed his head in her direction and played it again.

She clapped wildly when he was finished.

"It's a pleasure," he said. "I don't usually have such an appreciative audience."

"Yes you do, if you're in the same room with yourself," I muttered. But even if they had heard me, they paid no attention.

They were beaming at each other. What a great deal Beth and Douglas have in common, I reflected bitterly. They both think Douglas is wonderful.

I thought back to a week ago, when I'd been worried that Beth would have found our house crazy and cluttered and my family likewise. That had certainly been a foolish worry. Beth was far too blinded by the Hoffmans' various geniuses to notice the Hoffmans' hideous environment.

Did she even remember I was there?

Why should she?

"And this is Laura. She's twelve."

More than ever I felt the intense need to be able to do something, *anything* that would make me shine in the midst of all those stars. Now it wasn't only my family that I felt didn't notice me —it was Beth too.

Was it always going to be this way? Would I spend my life being "and this is Laura" while the rest of my family went about the business of being famous?

If only I could see into the future! If only I could catch a glimpse of what tomorrow, next week, next year had in store for me. Perhaps I would find out that life wouldn't always be this way, that things would change, that *I* would change, that something would happen that would alter the course of my whole life. Maybe I would find out that I was destined for great things, in spite of how remote that possibility now seemed.

But of course the whole idea was ridiculous. No one could foretell what the future would bring. It just wasn't possible.

5

It was at dinner that it happened for the first time.

Jill was chattering away about Mr. Kane and what we could expect from the drama club, and Beth was listening intently while shoveling forkfuls of Moroccan chicken and rice into her mouth. Dennis murmured a running monologue about how in fifteen years of marriage my mother had never wrecked the rice, while my mother vainly protested that she'd been married twenty years, and her wrecked rice record was second to none. Douglas was jotting down notes for a debate on whether the Chinese or American system of education was more efficient and trying to wangle my father into an argument about it. My father insisted that he knew nothing about either system.

Beth seemed so at home there, right in the center of the conversation. She leaned forward on her elbows, absorbing Jill's every word. It was funny how instantly comfortable I'd been in her house and how easily she'd fit into mine, when our families were so dissimilar.

At that moment I felt more out of it than ever. It was like I was a tiny desert island in the midst of a huge, bustling metropolis. Even my chair was a little farther away from the table than anyone else's. I was a person apart.

And then the entire scene seemed to fade from my consciousness and instead I saw a picture in my mind of a place filled with glass jars, bubbling beakers, tubes—all kinds of scientific equipment. Reality disappeared entirely. I didn't hear any of the voices around me, didn't see my family seated at the table, knew nothing but that I was looking into a well-equipped laboratory.

The picture got clearer and clearer, like when you're focusing binoculars, and I saw my father standing in the middle of all that apparatus looking hopelessly lost.

Then another figure appeared in the picture— a man wearing a white shirt. He spoke to my father briefly and the next thing I knew my father was clapping his hand to his head and jumping into the air with a huge smile on his face.

The picture dissolved.

I was back at the table; it was still dinnertime.

Jill was still talking. Everything was exactly the same.

I looked around, frowning. What in the world had happened? What was that I had just seen? What did it mean, and how did I happen to see it? It was much too vivid to have been a daydream. Besides, if I was going to daydream about anything it would have been something a lot more exciting than my father's lab.

"Come on, Dad," said Douglas. "You must have some opinions on what they're doing in China."

My father looked annoyed. "I can't have opinions on something I know nothing about. Now, please, Doug, I have a lot on my mind, and I really don't—"

"You'll figure it out tomorrow," I blurted out. "After the man in the white shirt comes."

I dropped my fork.

Everyone but Dennis turned to stare at me. Dennis muttered something about getting your clothes whiter than white.

Now what in the world had made me say such a thing? How did I know what that picture in my mind had meant? How did I know when, if ever, that scene was going to happen? What made me say tomorrow?

I snatched my fork and began stuffing rice into my mouth. Suddenly they were all on me at once. "What are you talking about? How do you know? Figure *what* out?"

I was completely confused. I had no idea what to tell them; I had no idea myself what I was talking about. I tried to use a full mouth as an excuse not to answer but I was rapidly running out of rice.

They wouldn't leave me alone. When my plate was entirely clean I forced myself to look up at all those questioning faces.

"What did you mean?" my father asked. I shrugged.

"What man in a white shirt?" Jill persisted.

"Just a man."

"Because a man likes to feel like a *man*," Dennis warbled.

"Stop being so mysterious," Douglas ordered. "Are you going into the prediction business?"

"Can you predict things?" Beth gasped.

I glanced her way. She looked absolutely awestruck. She was staring as if she'd never seen me before. Her mouth was slightly open and she seemed to be in unbearable suspense as she awaited my reply.

How impressed they'd all be, I thought, if I *could* predict things. They'd be hanging on my every word. No one would make a move without consulting me first. Being able to foretell the future was just about the most amazing talent anyone could have. Compared to that, piano playing, bowling and acting were mere child's play. And as for scientific geniuses—well, not even a scientific genius would be able to figure out how to see into tomorrow.

"Can you?" Beth repeated.

Instead of saying, "No, of course I can't predict things," I replied, "I don't know."

Well, I *didn't* know. I'd never predicted anything before; I'd never had a *vision* come into my mind that way before.

"Well what were you talking about?" my mother asked.

"Oh, just a hunch."

My father searched my face like he was looking for clues.

"How did you know I had to figure something out?"

I didn't want to lie, but I also didn't want to break the web of mystery I seemed to have woven around myself. So I just shrugged. My father's juggling had been a dead giveaway that he was struggling with something, not to mention his impatience with Douglas; but at the moment I was enjoying the unaccustomed attention too much to give it up. It was nice to be noticed. Even nicer than I imagined.

After school the next day I went home with Beth. She'd wanted to go to my house but I convinced her that it would be better if we went to hers. Since the first time I'd been there I had been eager to go back. It seemed to me like a haven from my own family, the promise of a couple of hours of calm and quiet, the soothing orderliness of well-tended rooms and well-dressed people.

It wasn't that hard to convince her. Beth had been nagging me about my prediction ever since dinner the night before. It almost seemed to have made her forget about my mother's book. Right through school she kept it up, whenever she saw me. Could I really see the future? Could I see *her* future? Would I *try* to predict something that would happen to her? Could I do it now? Maybe this afternoon?

I told her that I didn't know; I'd have to wait and see. You couldn't force these things, I said. Well, I really had no idea whether or not you could force these things, but I hadn't seen anything more the night before, no matter how hard I tried to, so I supposed you couldn't.

But I had a feeling, I said, that a nice, quiet house like hers would make it easier to concentrate on the Beyond. . . .

It was not the maid's day, and Beth's mother wasn't home yet. Roger arrived shortly after we did. Beth was responsible for him until Mrs. Traub returned from work.

"He's in one of his moods," said Beth, rolling her eyes.

He was starving. He hadn't eaten any lunch because he'd forgotten his lunch money and no one would give him anything, not even one little potato chip.

"You have to make me lunch," he told Beth.

"I'm not going to make you lunch," she objected. "It's too late for lunch now. You can have a snack."

"I don't want a snack," Roger whined. "I want lunch. *I didn't have any lunch.*"

"All right, all right. You certainly *sound* hungry enough. I'll make you a peanut butter sandwich."

"I don't want a peanut butter sandwich. They had pizzaburgers for lunch today." He looked desolated.

"Forget it, Roger," Beth said harshly. "It's peanut butter or nothing."

"Beth," I whispered, "the poor kid is starving. Don't be so mean."

"Listen, you know how many times he forgot his lunch money? And it's always me who has to start making him a lunch at three-thirty. He just does it to get attention. That's why no one will give him anything any more. The first couple of times everyone felt sorry for him, and he ate like a king. This kid gave him pretzels, that kid gave him his first fruit salad, this kid gave him a Ring Ding—he ate better than if he'd had his own lunch. After the first eight times, they got wise to him."

"Look, get me some celery." She shrugged and got out a bunch of celery. I spread peanut butter over two stalks. Then she got an apple and a piece of American cheese at my direction. I cut the apple into quarters and the cheese into four triangles. Roger watched me, fascinated.

"One piece of bread," I ordered, "and some jelly." I spread jelly on the bread and cut it into three strips. I arranged all this on a plate and handed the plate to Roger.

He gazed at it. He looked up at me as if I were some kind of wizard.

"That's nice," he said softly. "Thank you."

He walked out of the room carrying the plate very carefully.

Beth stared after him.

"That's the first time I ever heard that kid say thank you."

"I do that for Dennis sometimes," I said. "Little kids like things cut up that way. Makes the food more interesting, I guess."

"Well, thanks a heap. You got him off my back for a while anyway. Now you can have all the quiet you need to concentrate. Come on up to my room where you won't be disturbed."

"I'll try," I said a few minutes later as I sprawled out on her bed with a throw pillow to prop me up. "But I'm not promising anything."

I closed my eyes and tried to concentrate. The harder I tried to see something, to get a picture in my mind like the one I'd had last night, the less I saw. In fact, I didn't see anything. "Think, think" was all that kept running through my head, but nothing was there to think about.

I opened my eyes, which had gotten tighter and tighter as I tried to force a "vision" and found Beth staring at me expectantly.

"Well?"

"Nothing's . . . coming through."

"Last night you were right in the middle of everything when you came up with it. Maybe it's *too* quiet here."

She might be right. I remembered the feeling of being surrounded by a bunch of people chattering with each other and paying no attention to me. I remembered how out of it I'd felt. I recalled the sensation of being a person apart, of not fitting in.

"Hmm. You might have something there."

Beth went out of her room and leaned over the stairs.

"Roger!" she yelled. "Turn the television louder!"

A moment later the sound of the TV grew fainter.

"Roger! I said *louder!*"

"*Louder?*" he yelled back.

"YES!"

The television blasted through the house.

"He's going to go deaf listening to it like that," I warned.

"Don't worry; it's only for a little while."

She opened her instrument case and took out her flute. She turned her back to me and tweetled loudly enough to be heard over the blare of the TV.

It was awful. Absolutely hideous. It was even worse than being in my own house. The flute shrieked and squealed. A cartoon character screamed lisping threats to his archenemy while in the background someone operated a whining buzzsaw accompanied by howls of shrill, cackling laughter.

Desperately I put my hands to my head and tried to tune out the din. I didn't think I could stand much of this—in another moment I'd be shrieking myself, begging Beth to let me out of this madhouse so I could go home to my own madhouse. I pressed my fingers against my temples and closed my eyes. It was too much, too much, this would never work, I couldn't—

Beth was standing on a big stage. She was all alone and a spotlight was shining on her. She looked beautiful. Her blond hair was a cloud around her face. She was wearing some kind of long robe or dress and there were baskets of flowers heaped at her feet. Her face was glowing with joy. Her eyes shone out at an invisible presence beyond my vision. Humbly she bowed her head.

"PUT THAT DOWN! YOU PUT THAT DOWN! S-s-shufferin' shuccotash, I'll—"

My eyes flew open.

I sat bolt upright on the bed and pressed my hand to my chest. I couldn't believe it. Had I really—

Beth must have heard me sit up or something, because the tweetling stopped and she whirled around. One look at me and she shrieked, "You got something! You got something! Oh, Laura, what is it?"

I held my head. "Turn the TV down. Oh, please, turn it off." My head was pounding.

Beth raced downstairs. Almost instantly the TV became barely audible and she raced back upstairs and flung herself next to me on the bed.

"What was it? *Tell me.*" She clutched my hand, squeezing my fingers till I thought they'd fall off.

What was it I'd seen? Beth on stage. Getting flowers. Was she taking a bow? What did it mean? It seemed very simple. Beth was going to be an actress. No—no she didn't look any older. She looked just like she looked now, only dressed up, more elegant. It must be the club play.

"You're going to be the star of the play," I said.

"Oh, *Laura!*" Then she dropped my hand. "Oh, Laura, that's impossible. It can't be true."

"Well," I said, "that's what I saw. I don't know . . ."

I shrugged. My head was clear now and it didn't hurt. The vision, if that's what it was, had been just as vivid as the one I'd had last night. I didn't know when it would happen or if it would happen. The only thing I did know was that I had seen it, and it *wasn't* just my imagination.

"I can't believe it," Beth went on. "I can't believe it. Oh, Laura, do you really think it's going to happen?"

"Well," I hesitated. "I saw it very clearly."

That was certainly true.

"This is amazing," Beth raved. "Laura, you're *incredible*. Have you seen anything for yourself?"

"No. Maybe it only works for other people's futures."

That sounded kind of odd, but Beth didn't dwell on it. She urged me to try again, to see if I could see anything else, but I refused.

Once a day was enough, I told her. It took a lot out of me. What I didn't tell her was that I didn't know what it *was* that I was doing once a day; I didn't know what, if anything, it would take out of me. Not to mention the fact—which I didn't— that so far nothing had happened to prove that I actually *was* foretelling the future.

Beth's mother drove me home at five. I let myself in the front door and found my parents, Jill, and Douglas seated in the living room. They looked like they were ready to pounce on me, and in fact, when I came in they all started shouting at once.

I actually began to back out of the room when my father raised his hand and yelled louder than anyone else, "PLEASE!"

"What is it?" I asked. "Did I do something? Why are you all—"

"Laura," my father said gently, "an interesting thing happened to me today. Hacker—you know, I've mentioned him before—well, Hacker came down to see me about one of my requisition forms that he couldn't read. All day I'd been working on that problem of mine and getting nowhere. It wasn't two minutes after he left that it hit me. I did figure it out. Just like *that*." He snapped his fingers.

I stood there, with them all staring at me, and stared back.

It was true? I had really looked into the future? I had really seen what was going to happen? I shook my head in disbelief. If I didn't sit down, I realized, I was likely to collapse on the spot. My legs were trembling.

'Hacker," said my father, "was wearing a white shirt. And a red tie."

I gripped the arm of the sofa with one hand and leaned against it. My brain was reeling and the room seemed to tilt sideways. I said the first silly thing that came into my head.

"I didn't notice the tie."

6

"I'm sure you're all anxious to get on with the auditions," said Mr. Kane, "but before we start I want to give you a little information on what you're getting yourselves into, so no one can complain later. Rehearsals for our play will be held at least twice a week, sometimes more, depending on how things go. You'll be expected to have your parts memorized in two weeks. Every member of the cast should attend all rehearsals. Anyone who misses more than three rehearsals is out.

"You've had a chance to read the play and to pick out the roles you'd like to try. Obviously you're not all going to get the parts you want, so don't be too disappointed if you have to take your second or third choice. There will be other plays."

Beth could barely contain her impatience. She kept leaning forward, as if ready to spring up out of her seat and then, as Mr. Kane kept talking, would slump back again and sigh. She was going to try out for the lead.

I don't know if that was because the prediction about my father had come true, or because I kept telling her what a good actress she was; maybe it was both. On the one hand she couldn't believe she was talented enough to be chosen to star over Jean Freeman. On the other hand I *had* been right about my father and the man in the white shirt.

I was almost as nervous as she was. Naturally I wasn't going to try out for the starring role, but I'd decided on a nice minor character who didn't have too many lines to speak. It wasn't a very demanding part and I didn't think anyone else would even bother to audition for it. Beth had insisted that I try out for something so we could be in the play together and since I was well aware of my own limitations, I was satisfied to start small.

The two boys who had come to the first drama club meeting had disappeared into thin air, never to return again. Consequently Mr. Kane had found a play that required only girls. It wasn't a great play, but it wasn't bad either. It was called *The Phantom of Sigma Phi*. It took place in a sorority house (naturally) in college, and was a sort of a comedy-mystery-melodrama-thriller. There were mysterious goings-on, weird telephone

62

calls, girls disappearing, lights turning on and off with strange effects—which gave our stage and lighting crew a great deal of satisfaction—and, very possibly, a couple of hauntings.

The whole thing is closely connected to the annual intersorority basketball championship, which a rival sorority is determined to win by fair means or foul.

I was sure Beth would be perfect in the starring role. But the other reason that I was nervous was because if my prediction was accurate and she got the part I wasn't sure that I wouldn't faint. Yet if she didn't get the part she might blame me for getting her hopes up for nothing. And it might mean that I couldn't see the future after all.

Mr. Kane finally stopped talking and called for the first bunch of people to read for the part Beth wanted. I gave her hand an encouraging squeeze. She whispered, "Eek!" only half-kiddingly and widened her eyes and mouth in mock terror.

About eight girls wanted to audition for the main part, including Jean Freeman and Rita Lovett. Mr. Kane had them all read the same lines. Rita was awful. Most of the other girls weren't that good either, except for a girl named Sonia Bibby, but it was obvious that Beth and Jean Freeman were the best. You couldn't tell what Mr. Kane thought because he said the same thing to everyone who read. "Very good. Next, please." He made notes on a big yellow pad.

After everyone had finished reading for the part

of Eloise he said, "Those who want to read for Phyllis please come up."

"Mr. Kane!" Rita cried, "When will we find out if we got the part?"

"I'll post the cast list on my door tomorrow."

Beth took her seat and fanned her face with her hand. "I won't hold out till tomorrow," she whispered. "I was so *nervous*."

"You were super," I said. "I never would have known you were scared."

"You didn't," she said hopefully, "happen to get any more—uh—predictions while I was up there, did you?"

I shook my head.

When everyone had had a chance to read for the major roles Mr. Kane said, "Okay, that's it. Check my door tomorrow morning, then start memorizing your parts as soon as you can. We'll have our first run-through on Friday in here. Be sure and bring your scripts."

Beth looked at me, shocked. "But you didn't get a chance to try out for Nancy's part."

I was as surprised as she was. I couldn't understand why Mr. Kane had ended the auditions.

"Mr. Kane," she called out, "what about the other parts?"

"I'll assign them," he said, "to some of the people who don't get the major roles."

"You mean, only the people who auditioned for the big parts will be in the play?"

"That's right."

"But we didn't know that," Beth said. And before I realized what she was going to say she went on, "Because Laura wanted to read for Nancy and she didn't get a chance."

Mr. Kane looked in my direction. I wished Beth hadn't made such a fuss about it. Sure, I was a little disappointed, but not that much, since it was only at her insistence that I'd agreed to try out for anything.

"I didn't realize that," Mr. Kane said. "All right, Laura, why don't you come on up and read Nancy's lines on page"—he checked over the script—"thirteen. And anyone else who didn't understand how the tryouts would work and who didn't get a chance, come up front and you can read for the parts you want."

I made my way down the center aisle and climbed up the steps to the stage. I wished Beth had kept her mouth shut. The stage seemed huge and I felt very small and lonely being the only person on it.

I wasn't scared so much as embarrassed. I realized as I read my few lines, remembering to "Pro*ject*," as Mr. Kane had told everyone, that they sounded ridiculous and hardly required any acting ability at all. The other parts had much longer speeches, so when you read them you really had something substantial to read. But the role of Nancy had no speech longer than two lines, so what I was reciting was all jerky and disconnected.

"Meat loaf *again*," I read, trying to sound disgusted.

"Who was that on the phone?"

"This library book is two years overdue."

It was impossible. Even a great actress couldn't have made much out of a bunch of one-liners like that and I certainly wasn't in the great actress category. I'd made a big mistake in reading that part at all, because I probably sounded even less talented than I was.

"Very good," said Mr. Kane, noncommittal as ever. "Next."

I went back to my seat and slumped down next to Beth. A few more people had followed me toward the stage and were waiting for their turns.

"I never should have done it," I whispered miserably to her. "That was awful."

"No it wasn't," she whispered back. She patted my hand. "You were fine."

"I wasn't fine. I was terrible."

"It was the part you did, it wasn't your fault. It's not a very exciting part, that's all. You were just right."

"Yeah, I was unexciting too."

"Well, that's the role you wanted. You should have tried for a better one."

Mr. Kane must be discouraged, I thought, after expecting to find another Jill in his club, to realize that just because my name is Hoffman it didn't mean that I would follow in my sister's footsteps.

But of course, that's what I'd been trying to do. Why had I joined the drama club in the first place, if not to see if I could be like my sister? Why had I stayed in the club, when I realized right away that I was not very good at dramatics? Why had I tried out for this play at all?

By the time we left the auditorium, it was all settled as far as I was concerned.

"I'm not going to be in the club anymore," I told Beth as I walked her to the bus.

"Laura, you can't quit now!"

"Why not? I should have quit three weeks ago. There's no point to it. I can't act and it's just a big waste of time."

"At least wait and see if you get the part," Beth insisted. "You can't try out for something and then not do it."

"I won't get the part," I said. "Don't worry about that."

"At least wait and see," she repeated. "Wait till tomorrow morning before you make up your mind."

"My mind is made up, but I won't go running after Mr. Kane and hand in my resignation this minute, if that's what you mean. I won't go to any more meetings, that's all."

"I was really looking forward to our being in the play together," Beth sighed. "It would have been fun."

"I'm sorry. But it isn't fun for *me*."

She paused on the bottom step of the bus. "Let's just see what happens tomorrow."

Only Jill seemed to be home when I got in. She was pacing up and down the living room, a script in one hand and a banana in the other. She was mumbling as she paced, even as she nibbled at the banana.

"Don't tell me," I said. "It's a new speech improvement technique. Like Demosthenes with the pebbles in his mouth, right?"

She laughed. "No, just memorizing. I'll tell you, though, it wouldn't hurt this play a bit if I did the whole thing with a mouthful of banana. It's a perfectly dreadful play and I have a perfectly dreadful part and the whole thing is going to be a complete fiasco. I don't know what got into Ms. Malone, picking a play like this."

"So why don't you stay out of it?"

Jill gave me a blank look. "I can't," she said simply. "I've got the lead."

"Oh. Of course." I flopped down on the couch and put my legs over the armrest. "I'm quitting the drama club."

She stopped pacing and turned to face me. "Why? What's the matter?"

"I can't act, that's what's the matter. And I'm tired of that hopeless look on Mr. Kane's face all the time. Like I'm a constant disappointment to him because I don't take after you. He expected me to be brilliant and I've turned out to be lousy."

"Oh, Laura, you're exaggerating."

Why did everyone keep denying what I could see as plainly as my own shoes? First Beth, now Jill insisted I couldn't possibly be as untalented as I knew I was. It was very annoying. Even Mr. Kane didn't really want to believe it, despite the mounting evidence.

"I'm not exaggerating. I tried out for a part in the play today and I was awful. And I couldn't do pantomime, and I read my monologue terribly, and—"

"Do it for me," Jill interrupted. "Do the part you tried out for."

I reached into my looseleaf for the script. Jill sat down on the floor next to the couch. "What did you read?"

"Page thirteen. Nancy's lines."

She flipped through the pages till she found the spot.

"Why in the world did you read that?" She turned some more pages and skimmed over lines until she got to the part Beth had read.

"Do this."

I took the script from her hand and held it up so I could read it on my back.

"Stand up," she ordered. "You can't act lying down."

"You can if you're in an X-rated movie."

"You're a bit young to be rehearsing for that," she retorted. "Now get up and read it."

I hauled myself off the couch. I stood in front

of Jill, in the middle of the room and read the lines. I really tried.

"It needs work," she said, when I'd finished. "But you're not nearly as lousy as you think you are. I could help you."

"Thanks, but no thanks. I'm not cut out for this. And two actresses in the family are enough."

"All right, you do whatever you want. But I don't want you to quit because you think you're no good. With a little training—"

"I'd be mediocre instead of lousy," I finished.

"Anybody home, I hope?" my mother yelled from the kitchen.

"Not mediocre," Jill corrected, "fine. We're in here!"

"Well come on in *here* and help me unload this stuff."

We went into the kitchen and followed my mother out the back door to the station wagon, where about fifty-nine bags of groceries and Dennis were piled in the middle seat.

"Come on out, Dennis," my mother said. "We're home."

"I can't," he said. "I'm stuck."

He was surrounded on all sides by bags.

"Mother, why didn't you put the stuff in the back?" Jill asked. "He can't move."

My mother gave her a steely glare. "I *did*," she replied. "If you'd care to look there are about a hundred and two more bags in the back. And I'm in no mood for criticism, Jill dear. I have just spent a harrowing two-and-a-half hours."

We ferried groceries into the kitchen and Dennis finally emerged from the car.

"I was trapped," he said grimly.

"Don't talk about trapped to me," my mother told him. "You just go into your room and count or something, because we are getting on each other's nerves."

"You're not getting on my nerves," he said. But he left.

She sank into a kitchen chair. "I think he did a commercial for every single thing I put in my basket. Not to mention all the things he wanted me to put in my basket that I didn't buy. At first they thought he was cute. Little old ladies stopped to listen to him. But he kept going—on and on and *on*. He didn't stop for two hours. People stared. I got the most pitying looks from mothers whose children were just throwing tantrums or knocking cans of peas off shelves. I finally couldn't stand it any more, so I sat him on an empty checkout counter and shoved a magazine in his hand and told him not to move. And ten minutes later I found him in the detergents and cleansers, pushing a cart piled high with cereal and potato chips and Ti-Dee Bowl. I can't imagine why he wanted fourteen packages of Ti-Dee Bowl."

"But why did you take him?" asked Jill. "You could have known—"

"Jill. *Dear*." My mother's voice was strained. "I

got involved with the portrait of Linnet's grand-mother and before I knew it he was home from school and I hadn't done the shopping and all we had in the house was a heel of bread and a desiccated lime."

"And a banana," I reminded her. She gave me the same kind of look she'd given Jill. "Sorry," I said meekly.

"But what did you do with all that stuff he took?" asked Jill.

"What did I do with it? I did nothing with it. I grabbed him by the arm and ran like hell." Her expression defied us to find fault with her behavior. *"Never* again."

I put a box of pizzas into the freezer. The cold air vapor was swirling like steam and then I didn't feel the cold at all. I didn't feel anything, not heat nor chill nor my hand clutching the handle of the freezer. All I could see was that fog, till my vision was completely obscured by it. Then it began to clear, and when I could see again I was not seeing stacks of frozen food on metal shelves, but a small room, like a child's room, with a little bed and a little rocking chair and a shelf of dolls.

My mother appeared in the middle of the room. She was dressed in what looked like a little girl's dress, but it was my mother's face and she was her adult size. She went over to the shelf and got a boy doll, which she placed on the rocking chair. Then she took a smaller doll, a girl, and put it next to the boy. Then another girl doll, smaller than the second, so the three dolls were lined up on the rocker. She reached up for a fourth doll, but it wasn't there.

She turned all the way around, surveying the whole small room. She ran to the bed, looked over and under it, ran back to the shelf and skimmed her hand over it to make sure she wasn't imagining the empty space. She counted the dolls on the rocker, pointing to each one with her finger.

Then she threw herself on the bed, which was too small for her, and started pounding her fists into the pillow and kicking her feet wildly.

". . . close that freezer door!"

I was peering at a shelf full of frozen vegetables. I slammed the door shut. I didn't turn around right away, but leaned against the freezer, too shaken to move.

What I had seen had been grotesque, full of a sense of vague menace. My mother, in a child's pinafore, playing with dolls, a weird figure in a weird room. And then, the lost doll, the temper tantrum, all of which I had watched but not heard, since there had been no sound at all throughout the entire scene.

"What's wrong with you? Laura?" Jill grasped me by the shoulders and turned me around. "I'll bet she's had another hunch. Haven't you, Laura?"

I shook my head. "No, no, it's nothing."

"Laura, what is it?" My mother got up and

came over to where I was still leaning against the freezer. "Are you all right?"

"Yeah, sure. I'm fine. It's nothing. I didn't see anything."

"What do you mean, you didn't see anything?" Jill demanded.

"Nothing, just a figure of speech."

What I had seen became even more frightening as I gradually discovered what it had to mean. Instead of being pleased that I could interpret my vision, instead of dissolving the feeling of dread that it had brought with it, I found that when I was sure of what it meant, I was more terrified than ever.

Because of course, the missing doll was Dennis.

7

I slept badly that night; in fact, I hardly slept at all.

I was afraid to close my eyes, for fear that I might have another "vision." Maybe it was the idea of my mind going off and thinking up things on its own, over which I had no control, that I found so scarry. Even the thought of dreaming was terrifying.

The possibility of something bad happening to Dennis was enough in itself to keep me awake, because that was the only explanation for what I had seen. The Dennis doll was missing and my mother had gotten hysterical over it. No matter how hard I thought—and I had plenty of time to think through that long night—there was no other way to interpret it. *Something was going to happen to Dennis.*

But was it really a prediction? So far the only evidence there was about my ability to see the future was the episode with my father and Hacker. We didn't know yet whether Beth was going to be the star of the play; it was still possible that I could be wrong about that. If only I was wrong! That would mean I might be mistaken about Dennis, too.

I was groggy and bleary-eyed when I got to school the next morning but I was there practically as soon as they opened the doors. I raced down the hall to Mr. Kane's room and fought my way through the cluster of girls at the door. They were also impatient to see the cast list. But none of them had as good a reason to read that list as I did, and I elbowed my way to the front of the group, not caring about the grumbles and the shoves I received on the way.

Beth was right in front of the door and as I pushed myself next to her she turned to me, her face grim and accusing.

"I didn't get it," she said. "You were wrong."

I was flooded with feelings of relief, which must have shown on my face, because she said bitterly, "Well, you don't have to look so happy about it."

I felt terribly disloyal, being so glad that she hadn't gotten the part she wanted, but I couldn't help it. If I was wrong about this, then I could be wrong about Dennis, and that was more important than one Junior High School play.

I checked the list myself, just to make sure.

"Eloise: *Jean Freeman.*"

"Hey, Laura," someone said, "You got the part."

"I looked around to see who'd said it. "What part?"

"Nancy," Sonia Bibby replied. "The one you tried out for."

"I did?"

I looked at the list again. There it was, down near the bottom of the paper. "Nancy: *Laura Hoffman.*"

"I don't believe it." I read the whole list with more interest now, and saw that Beth's name was second.

"Beth, you got the second lead! That's practically as good as Jean's part!"

Beth separated herself from the crowd and moved a little way down the hall. I followed her, not knowing whether I should feel happy or guilty or disappointed or what. It was bewildering.

"Beth, now we'll be together in the play, just like you wanted."

"You said I was going to be the star," she said. "And you didn't want to be in it anyway. Just yesterday you said you were going to quit the club."

"But you told me I couldn't if I got the part. Beth, I'm sorry about what I told you. I never should have said it. But you wanted to know, and you kept insisting and insisting that I try to see something for you. Maybe that's not what it meant. Maybe it meant that you'd be so good, you'd steal the show and end up being the star."

"That's not what you said."

"Look, I'm new at this. I told you I couldn't be sure of being right."

"I know." She put her flute case into her locker and pulled out some books. "It's just—well, I really psyched myself up for that part. And why did you have to look so happy when you found out I didn't get it?"

"Beth, I'm sorry. It wasn't that I was glad you didn't get the part; it was that I was glad I was wrong."

And I told her the whole thing.

The look of shock on her face when I explained what the dolls meant was enough to convince me that she wasn't angry anymore.

"No wonder you were so happy! It must have been awful lying awake the whole night waiting to find out."

Suddenly a shadow crossed her face and she frowned. She bent toward her locker and started fooling with more books.

"Beth, what is it? What were you just thinking?"

"Nothing."

"Beth!"

She turned to face me. Her eyes darkened and

she gnawed at her lip a moment before she replied.

"All right," she said finally. "All right. What does it prove?"

"What do you mean, what does it prove? I was wrong."

"*Once.*"

"Yeah, but—"

"And you were right once. So far your score is fifty-fifty. How do you know which it is this time?"

Jamie Arons sat behind me in homeroom. As I slid into my seat, still disturbed by Beth's reasoning, she tapped me on the back.

"Are you really psychic, Laura?"

Startled, I blurted out, "How did you—" then stopped myself. But it was too late.

"I happened to hear you and Beth talking," she said innocently, "and at first I couldn't figure out what you were talking about. But then it hit me. Laura's psychic, I said to myself. That's the most fantastic thing I ever heard."

The look of admiration on her face almost, but not quite, made me forget about Dennis.

"Well," I said vaguely, "it is and it isn't."

"Oh, how can you say that? It's absolutely phenomenal. Why, there isn't one person in a million who can tell the future and here's someone in my own school, in my own homeroom, with the Gift. Think of it!"

Her eyes shone with excitement.

"But I'm not sure I can really—"

"Just because you're not always right doesn't mean you haven't got the Gift," Jamie said with great certainty. "I read this book, *The Weird World of Psychic Experience*—did you read that?"

I shook my head.

"It tells all about people like you. People who have precognition—" She stopped, seeing the puzzled look on my face.

"Precognition. That's 'knowing before.' It means like seeing things before they happen. Anyway, lots of times they aren't exactly right. Nobody's one hundred percent perfect, and you know why they're not always right?"

I shook my head, feeling almost hypnotized by her description of "people like me."

"Because lots of times they're not sure of what it is they're seeing. They misunderstand it, or they don't understand it at all. And it isn't until later, after the thing actually happens, that they realize what it meant."

I let this sink in for a minute. "Then you could see something and it would never really happen, but you were right anyway?" I was beginning to get confused.

"Well, look, you're not *always* right. Nobody is. But, for instance, there was this college girl who saw her boyfriend in a huddle with his football team and suddenly this giant, golden bird comes along and sinks his blood-red claws into her boyfriend's shoulders and lifts him right out of the huddle and flies off with him in his talons."

"That's horrible!" I shuddered.

"Yeah, that's what she thought. She was scared to death. She was so upset for days afterwards that she couldn't tell him about it. She was sure it meant he was going to die horribly, or be in a plane that was hijacked when the team was flying to a game. So she finally worked up her courage to tell him, and he laughed and laughed. And she said, 'What's so funny?' And he said, 'Well, I had something to tell you too. I've just been drafted by the Philadelphia Eagles.' "

"Good grief."

"Yeah. Here she thought something really bad was going to happen and it didn't turn out that way at all. So you don't always know."

"Well, that's a relief," I sighed. She certainly seemed to know what she was talking about, and it made a lot of sense. At least, if anything about this whole thing could make sense.

"But what do you suppose," I wondered, "that thing with the dolls could be?"

Jamie shrugged. "I don't know. That's the whole point. I'm just saying it doesn't necessarily have to mean something bad."

I took a big breath and exhaled loudly. I felt like someone had just removed a hundred bricks from my chest. "Boy, Jamie, you don't know how much better you made me feel."

"Good," she said. "Glad to help out. Now you can do something for me."

Even without that look of eager anticipation on her face, it wouldn't have been too hard to figure out what she wanted me to do for her.

"Give me a reading."

"A reading?"

"Yeah, read my future."

"Look, I'm not sure how much control I have over this. I don't know whether or not I can do it on demand."

"I know that," she said impatiently. "Goodness, you think I don't know that? All I'm asking you to do is try."

"Okay, I'll try." I really didn't have that much confidence in my ability at this point, and I couldn't help sounding doubtful. "But I can't guarantee anything."

Jamie came home from school with me that afternoon. Beth was dying to come too, but she had to stay for an orchestra rehearsal. She said she'd call me the instant she got home, to see if I'd been able to read something for Jamie.

Dennis greeted us at the door. So did the sound of the piano.

"I can't hear the television," Dennis said mournfully.

"I'm not surprised," I replied. "Why don't you watch in Mom and Dad's room?"

"Mom's writing. She won't let me watch there."

"So watch in Douglas's room."

"He says I can't use his television because I always break the channel turner."

"That's ridiculous. If he's going to bang away at that piano—"

I went over and tapped Douglas on the shoulder.

"What?" he asked, without stopping the music.

"Either stop playing that thing or let Dennis watch your T.V. You're not being fair."

"Life isn't fair," Douglas snapped. He kept on playing.

"Are you so wrapped up in your music that you aren't even aware of what's going on around you?"

"Yes."

"Good." I walked back to where Dennis was moping and leaned down to whisper in his ear. "Go up and watch his set. He'll never know the difference."

Dennis eyed me suspiciously.

"Go *ahead*," I insisted.

Without further urging he raced up the stairs.

Jamie giggled. I motioned her to follow me and we went up to my room. I closed the door, which shut out the sound of my mother's typewriter, but only slightly muffled the piano.

"He's cute," Jamie said.

"Which one?"

"Both of them, really. But I meant the little one."

"That's Dennis. The big one is Douglas.

I flopped onto my bed and gestured toward my desk chair for Jamie to sit down.

"How do you start?" she asked. "What do you have to do to see something?"

"I'm not sure. I'm not very experienced at this."

"Do you go into a trance?"

"I don't know," I repeated helplessly. "I think it sort of looks like I do."

"Well, do you want to keep talking or should I be quiet, or what?"

"I guess let's be quiet a minute and see if something happens."

I closed my eyes and tried to concentrate on Jamie. I waited. Nothing seemed to be happening. Jamie, Jamie, Jamie. I repeated her name over and over again in my head.

I suddenly felt as if I was in a goldfish bowl. My eyes snapped open and I saw that she was leaning forward eagerly in the chair, gazing at my face.

"Hey, read a book or something. I'm beginning to feel kind of self-conscious."

She went to my bookcase and grabbed a book without even looking at the title. She sat back down on the chair and opened the book at random. She peered down at the page, seeming to be absorbed in the story.

"Jamie," I said drily, "that's *My Golden Picture Dictionary*. It's Dennis's. I don't think you'll be too thrilled with the plot."

"Oh, what difference does it make? As long as

I'm not staring at you. Just pay no attention to me."

I took a deep breath and closed my eyes again. I began to feel terribly sleepy. And no wonder, since I'd hardly had any sleep the night before. Even with Douglas pounding the piano, I was more likely to doze off than to see Jamie's future, but I was so tired I didn't care. After all, I hadn't made any promises, except that I'd try, and in my condition she could hardly expect me to—

Jamie was dancing. She was wearing a floor-length velvet skirt in some dark color, and a white blouse. Her long, light brown hair was pulled tightly back from her face and held with a ribbon at the nape of her neck. I had never seen her wear it that way and it wasn't flattering. Otherwise she was lovely. She danced with her arms out and around an invisible partner. She had a dreamy, satisfied expression on her face. She turned so I could see her in profile. On the side of her forehead, right near her eyebrow, was a big red "A+" with a circle around it.

Instantly I was back in my room. I sat up on the bed, rubbed my eyes and frowned.

"What?" she demanded. "What was it? Tell me the whole thing."

"I'm not sure I didn't just fall asleep," I said, shaking my head. "I'm really exhausted. But—"

"But what?"

"No. No," I said, certain now. "I wasn't asleep.

I mean, it wasn't just a silly dream. Because it was like all the other ones."

"What was?" she cried. "What did you see?"

"It was really weird. I don't understand what it means at all."

"Laura!" She seemed ready to leap out of her chair and pounce on me.

"All right, all right." I told her.

She leaned back in the chair and wrinkled her forehead in concentration.

"What in the world could that mean?" she mused.

"I don't know. It was so crazy. And the minute I saw the 'A+' I woke right up again, so I'm sure that was the important thing."

"Maybe, maybe," she muttered. "And it was like a grade on a test?"

"Yeah, like with a red pen and circled, the way the teachers sometimes do it."

"A grade on my forehead . . ."

"Well, not exactly on your forehead, because I could only see it in profile. More like here." I pointed to my temple.

"Hmm." She chewed on her thumbnail while she pondered this.

"Maybe it means you have an A+ brain?" I suggested.

"No, that can't be it. That's not really a prediction so much as a character analysis. Anyway, I have a B— brain."

"Maybe you're going to get an A+ on a test or an important paper or something."

"Then why the dancing?"

I shrugged.

"This is going to drive me crazy. Here you actually manage to see something very important in my future and I can't even figure out what it is."

"It might not be all that important," I said. "Besides, I should be the one who tells you what it means. After all, I'm the one with the . . .Gift."

I liked the way that sounded! And I was beginning to believe that I really did have the Gift. After all, I was seeing *something* out of the ordinary, even if no one knew for sure what it was.

"Yeah, but you're new at it. You can't expect to be able to figure things out right away. You have to get a feel for it first. But I've read so much about this . . ." She shook her head.

"I'm really sorry, Jamie." I felt disappointed.

"Sorry? Why in the world should you be sorry? You were absolutely *miraculous*. It's just a matter of time before we come up with the true meaning, that's all. But you *did* it."

She got up and collected her books and her jacket. "And thank you," she added as we went downstairs.

"Oh, for nothing," I protested. "I didn't really tell you anything."

"Stop saying that!" She paused at the front door and looked me in the eye. "What you can do is *not* nothing. It's the most amazing thing in the world,

and only very special people are able to do it. It's a
rare gift, Laura, and don't you put yourself down."

"Well, thanks," I said, a little embarrassed.

"Thank *you*." I closed the door behind her.

The piano practice had stopped. Douglas
brushed past me carrying a huge sandwich and
was up the stairs before I realized what was bound
to happen.

At the sound of the shouting I finally recognized
a crisis in progress. I started to run up the steps.
Simultaneously, Douglas came charging down
them with his sandwich in one hand and a black
plastic channel selector from a television set in the
other. My mother emerged from her room like
she'd been shot out of a cannon, and Dennis
shrieked, "Laura *said!* Laura *said!*"

"Just where the hell do you get off telling him
he could use my set?" Douglas raged. "*I* told him
he couldn't. You know why? Because every time
he does he breaks it. This is the fourth time he's
broken it. And he really outdid himself this time.
Look at this. *Look* at it!"

"Douglas," my mother said. Her voice was full
of quiet menace. "*Douglas.*"

He whirled to face her. "What? *What?*"

"*Control yourself.*"

In the silence that followed Douglas took deep
breaths and glowered at me. Dennis piped shrilly,
"Didn't you say I could, Laura?"

"I did," I admitted. "There was no place else
for him to watch."

"You had no business telling him to use Douglas's set when Douglas said he couldn't. And you," she said, turning to Dennis, "could have done without television for half an hour. And you *certainly* didn't have to switch that channel selector back and forth and back and forth, since you know that's how it broke the last three times."

"I didn't switch it back and forth and back and forth. Douglas must have not fixed it very good."

"*I* must have—" Douglas started to howl.

"And so for your set," my mother cut in loudly, "if you can't fix it yourself this time, we'll take it to the repair shop and have them put a new tuner on, so you won't have this aggravation any more. The discussion is finished. Now I'm going to start dinner and I can use some help. Thank you for your cooperation."

She marched down the stairs, giving Douglas a little tap to get moving. He looked dazed. He never seemed to get used to my mother's bulldozer approach to family fights, even though he'd known her longer than any of us had except my father. She so seldom ordered us around that when she did, it always took Douglas by surprise.

It couldn't have been more than fifteen minutes later, while Douglas was grating potatoes, I was chopping onions, Dennis was peeling a carrot and my mother was hunting through every cabinet in the kitchen in search of cornstarch, when the phone rang.

Dennis dropped his carrot and grabbed for the

phone, jumping to reach the receiver because it's a little high on the wall for him.

"Hoffman residence. To whom did you wish to speak?"

"Why can't he just say hello like everyone else?" muttered Douglas.

"You taught him to say that," I pointed out, "back when he was a 'cute kid.' "

"We all make mistakes."

"It's for you, Laura."

"I wiped my hands on my jeans and took the receiver from him.

"Laura, this is Jamie. It's unbelievable. Sit down."

"What? What is?" Her voice was so charged with excitement I expected her to burst right through the phone and into the kitchen.

"Are you sitting down? I mean it, you better sit down. You're just not going to believe this."

"All right, all right." I stretched the long cord to the kitchen table and pulled out a chair. I sat down. "I'm sitting down. Now what is it?"

"Mark Temple just called and asked me to the ninth grade dance."

"What? I mean, that's nice, but—"

"Laura, think! Think! Dancing! A+ on the side of the head? Don't you get it?"

"Oh," I gasped, nearly dropping the phone onto the table. "A mark on the temple! *Mark Temple!*"

Even if I'd intended to keep the whole thing a secret from my family, Jamie's phone call would have blown it. You can't practically fall off a chair, gape like a fish gulping for air, and stagger a bit as you go to hang up the phone without people getting a little suspicious.

Dennis went right on peeling his carrot and crooning, "A carrot a *day* keeps the doctor *away*," but Douglas and my mother blocked my path back to the table.

"*Now*," my mother folded her arms across her chest, "what is going on?"

I tried to step around her but Douglas planted himself in front of me.

"All right," I gave in. "I'll tell you all about it. At dinner. I guess it's about time."

It *was* time. Now that there was no longer any doubt in my mind it was only fair that my family knew that I had the Gift. But instead of telling just the two of them, and then having to repeat the whole thing again, it would be better to wait until we were all together. I admit there might also have been something appealing in the picture of the entire family seated around the table, listening, fascinated, as plain, ordinary Laura revealed her astonishing newfound talent.

"All right," my mother agreed. "We'll wait till dinner."

"But don't you go running off to Tibet or something before then," Douglas warned.

"I have no intention of running off to Tibet before dinner, Douglas," I replied coldly.

The family was assembled, the pot roast and

potato pancakes had been dished out and Dennis, Jill and my father were eagerly digging in.

"Laura," my mother announced rather formally, "has something to tell us."

It was embarrassing, being introduced like that.

My father and Jill looked over at me, with almost identical expressions of polite concern. Dennis continued to stack slices of meat and potato pancakes on top of each other to make an imposing structure of food.

I cleared my throat self-consciously.

"It seems," I began, "that I'm psychic."

My father's fork stopped en route to his mouth.

Jill looked startled, but only for a second. "I knew it," she said. She smacked her palm against the table. "I *knew* it."

My mother frowned. Douglas just shot me a look of impatient disbelief.

Dennis said, "I need somebody to cut my meat."

Jill reached for his plate, briskly dismantled his meat and pancake tower and began cutting up the pot roast.

"All together!" Dennis yelled. "Cut it all together."

"Hush!" ordered Jill. "Didn't I know you were seeing things? Didn't I *say* that?"

"What makes you think you're psychic?" asked my father. "The thing with Hacker and my problem?"

"That was the first," I said.

"You mean there were others?" my mother asked. "You had other—hunches?"

"Yes. A couple."

"I knew it," Jill repeated. "I just knew it."

"A couple," mused my father. "How many?"

I told them. From the beginning, with the one about my father's lab, right up to the prediction about Jamie and Mark Temple. But I left out the vision of my mother and the dolls. I couldn't bring myself to make her any more worried than she already looked. In fact, my parents' and Douglas's reactions were not what I'd expected at all. Instead of gazing at me with awe and admiration, my mother and father looked as if they feared for my health. Douglas appeared utterly skeptical.

"So it's only three times actually that you've had these—whatever you want to call them," my father summed up.

"Yeah, right." Maybe three times wasn't so impressive after all. Maybe I should have waited until I had a whole string of predictions to tell them about.

"And of those three only two were even remotely accurate," Douglas pointed out.

"Two out of three ain't bad," Jill retorted.

"Insufficient evidence. Right, Dad?"

"I don't know. Let's see if we can find a rational explanation for these phenomena."

"You *have* a rational explanation," insisted Jill. "Laura is psychic."

"I meant an explanation that didn't depend on

supernatural beliefs. For instance, Laura, did you know that Jamie and Mark were interested in each other?"

"No. I hardly know Mark Temple at all and I really don't even know Jamie that well."

"And she never talked to you about him? Never gave you the idea that she'd like him to take her to this dance?"

"No, Dad, I told you, I hardly ever talked to her until today."

"Well, let's see. You know Beth is a good actress, so seeing her on a stage is not so strange."

"You don't have to explain that one," Douglas reminded him. "It didn't happen."

"It might," Jill said. "Just because it didn't happen immediately doesn't mean it won't ever happen."

"That's true," my father agreed, "if you accept any of this."

"Do you?" my mother asked. She looked intently at him. "Do you accept it?"

He shrugged. "I accept that it occurred. I accept that Laura saw—pictures, images, whatever —I just don't necessarily accept her interpretation of them as psychic phenomena."

"*I* do," said Jill. "It's not only Laura's interpretation. I interpret them that way too."

"If we're lining up sides," Douglas commented, "I'm with Dad."

"Don't you think," Jill demanded, "that even seeing visions is a little unusual, Douglas? I mean, leaving out the prediction part *entirely,* just for the sake of argument, it is not an ordinary thing to have visions."

"Daydreams," he scoffed. "Fantasies. Imagination. People do it all the time."

"They were not daydreams!" I cried, clanging my fork on my plate. Everyone was astonished at my outburst. Even Dennis looked up from the little tower of sliced carrots he was erecting.

Nothing was turning out as I'd expected. I was at last the center of attention, but instead of having all eyes focussed on me, instead of having five pairs of ears straining to absorb every word I said, they were practically dissecting me as if I weren't even in the room. (Well, that sounds ridiculous, but you know what I mean.)

Instead of marveling over me, instead of oohing an ah-ing and begging me to use my Gift for the good of mankind, instead of trying to help me cope with my incredible supernatural powers, they were bickering over whether or not I actually *had* them.

No, it was not at all the way I'd pictured it.

If my family's reaction left something to be desired, the reaction of the kids at school made up for it. Jamie had lost no time, it seemed, in telephoning eighty of her most intimate friends and telling them they had a Genuine Psychic in their midst. Then, each of the eighty must have telephoned eighty more, and so on, and all this was apparently accomplished by seven-thirty the next morning.

At first it was downright scary.

I barely walked into school and started down the hall to my locker when someone cried, "There she is!" and I was surrounded by a mob of kids all shouting at once.

"Hey," I whimpered. *"Hey."* I began to panic. Jamie's face emerged from among the throng. "Come on, you guys, give her room, she can't breathe, for heaven's sake!"

The crowd parted like the Red Sea. Dazed, I walked between two lines of people all clamoring for something or other and plucking at my jacket sleeves.

"What *is* this?" I gasped as Jamie led me toward our homeroom. "What are they after me for?"

"They're not after you," she corrected. "They just want you to give them readings. But I don't want you to do a thing until we have a chance to talk about it."

"Do a thing? About what? What readings? How did they—"

"Well, I was so excited about the reading you gave me, I told a couple of people. I guess word just got around."

"It sure got around fast. Jamie, I really wish you hadn't—"

I sank into my seat. They were still milling

about in front of the door like a swarm of bees discussing a rich new source of pollen.

"Don't get excited," said Jamie. "I'll handle everything."

She patted my shoulder reassuringly and strode to the door.

"Disperse, ye rebels," she commanded, with an imperious wave of her hand. It didn't work at Concord and it didn't work here, either. But I don't know what she did next, because at that very moment a small mob began to form around my desk and my view was blocked by another group of eager faces.

"Is it true?" Barry Cohen demanded.

"Do you really have ESP?" Steve Freeman asked.

"Laura, Laura!" Katie Quinn shook my shoulder urgently. "Laura, will I pass English?"

They all chattered away at me, ignoring or interrupting one another, everyone trying to be heard over the din everyone else was making. I could only pick out a question here and there and even when I did I couldn't answer. I hadn't had this much of a fuss made over me since my birthday in the first grade, when my father brought in cupcakes and did some juggling for the class.

"All right, all right," Jamie said, "break it up." She elbowed her way through the group to stand beside my chair. "This is ridiculous. You can't hassle Laura like this. She's sensitive."

I am?

"You'll all get a chance to talk with her."

They will?

"Just see me after school and I'll arrange it."

Arrange it? I looked questioningly at Jamie. She patted my shoulder again. I was not reassured.

"Take your seats, *please!*" Mrs. Ramirez had to practically scream to make herself heard, but finally the area around my desk was cleared of people.

I threw Jamie a desperate, pleading look as the bell rang.

"Don't worry," she hissed. "Leave everything to me."

Lunch was the first chance I got to talk to her. Beth was saving a seat for me and Jamie squeezed in on my right side as I sat down.

"Laura, you're famous!" Beth exclaimed. "The whole school knows about you. *I'm* even famous because I'm your friend."

"And this is just the beginning," Jamie declared.

"The beginning of what?" I twisted around to face her. "Jamie, what is all this you're planning for me? Don't I have a right to know?"

Before she could reply, the inevitable happened.

"Laura, you just *have* to tell me—" Katie Quinn again. And behind her, around her, swarming all over us, another mob.

"Good grief," Beth murmured.

"You can say that again," I wailed. I clapped my hands over my ears.

A lunchroom aide was bearing down on us, intent on discovering the cause of the disturbance.

"Now look!" Jamie yelled. "You're going to get us all in trouble. Will you please get out of here and see me after school. Laura can't do a thing for you now. All you're doing is draining her psychic energy."

The aide muscled her way to our table.

"What's going on here?"

Everyone scattered. The aide stared down at us. We looked back at her, our faces innocent. Her eyes scanned the whole table. Not finding a copy of *Playgirl* or bits of stray marijuana or anything else that might explain the commotion, she just shot us a menacing glare and barked, "Well, don't let it happen again!"

She marched away, seeking out more promising troublemakers.

Beth exhaled a long sigh of relief.

"*Now,* Jamie," I said, "you'd better tell me what you have in mind."

"Okay. I have it all figured out. You're going to give readings. Every day from four to five."

"She has play rehearsals," objected Beth.

"Well, okay, on the days she doesn't have rehearsals, then. I figure about a dollar a reading ought to be right—"

"Wait a minute! *Wait a minute!*" I was too

astounded to know which part of Jamie's wild scheme to protest first.

"You mean I'm going to charge money for this?"

"Of course. You have to. Otherwise you'll be just—*overwhelmed*. Now, figuring on the time you took to do mine, I think you ought to be able to squeeze in about ten people a day—"

"Ten people a day! I can't—"

"Eight then. We don't want to strain your powers."

"Hold it," I said firmly. "Hold it right there. Jamie, I never said I'd be able to give people predictions, let alone open a fortune-telling parlor."

"But you can, can't you?"

"Well, I don't know—maybe—I guess—"

"All right, then, we'll tell them maybe. I won't promise anything except that you'll try. And we won't guarantee accuracy. That way," she went on knowledgeably, "we can't be sued."

"Sued!"

"I said, *can't* be sued. Now, I'll make the appointments—"

"Maybe it would be easier," Beth said, "if you just did it on a first-come-first-served basis. You know, let everyone know that Laura will be reading from four to five and she can only take eight people and they can line up, and—"

"Beth!" I groaned.

"I don't know about that." Jamie wrinkled her

forehead. "Her parents might not be too thrilled about that kind of mob scene every day."

"They wouldn't!" I cried. "They wouldn't be thrilled at all. They would be very un-thrilled."

"Well, all right," Beth conceded. "Appointments, then. You could keep a little notebook," she suggested to Jamie.

It was all moving much too fast for me. Like Alice in *Through the Looking Glass*, I felt I had to run as fast I could just to stay in the same place. Only yesterday I had been plain old normal Laura and today I was a celebrity, with half the school practically clamoring to touch the hem of my garment. I was so confused I couldn't think straight, which was probably why Jamie was able to push me around like a Tonka toy.

"Jamie." I made a feeble attempt at objecting. "Beth. I don't think I want to do this. The whole idea makes me kind of nervous."

"Nervous about what?" Jamie demanded.

"I don't know—about charging money for it I guess—or maybe having to do it on demand—" I struggled to explain, but since I couldn't even explain my confused feelings to myself, I guess I didn't have much success making them clear to Beth and Jamie.

"I told you," Jamie said patiently, "that you *have* to charge money. That way you won't be hassled by thousands of kids with dumb questions that really aren't worth answering. If it costs money they'll only come to you for important things and there won't be as many people using up your time and energy."

"But I don't feel right charging for it."

"So give the money to charity," advised Beth. "You don't have to keep it if you don't want to."

"But you'd be crazy not to," said Jamie. "After all, you're performing a service. Doctors don't heal people for free. Ministers don't marry people for free. You have a great Gift—a talent—and you're entitled to cash in on it. Just like an artist sells his talent, or a piano player, or a—"

"All right, all right, I get the point!" Jamie could probably go on forever, reeling off examples of people who peddled their aptitude for profit. "But what if it doesn't work? What if I can't do it just like that every time someone asks for a reading?"

Jamie shrugged. "So you tried. What have you got to lose? Besides, with this kind of thing the more you use it the more highly developed it becomes. See, right now you're just a beginner, but as your psychic powers are exercised, they become stronger and stronger. Like muscles." She looked delighted at her comparison. "Just like muscles. The more you exercise them, the better they get. Which is another good reason for doing this. You don't want your Gift wasting away to nothing because you never use it, do you?"

"Well—no—I guess not." How could I want that? After longing for something that would make me special, something that would make my family proud of me, I couldn't just turn my back on my talent and let it dribble away—or whatever it was it would do if I didn't use it.

"Great," Jamie said, clapping her hands together briskly. "Leave everything to me."

"Laura," Beth breathed, "isn't this exciting? To think, when I first met you I had no idea you were going to be famous!"

"You think she's famous *now?* Huh, this is nothing. Stick with me, kid"—Jamie sounded like she was only half-joking—"and I'll get you on the Johnny Carson show."

"Jamie!" I shrieked. I was exhausted trying to keep up with all those big plans she had for me. "I don't *want* to be on the Johnny Carson show!"

"Okay." She shrugged. "Mike Douglas, then."

8

"All right, all right, keep it down!" Jamie's voice boomed over the excited chatter of the crowd on the staircase. "How do you expect Laura to concentrate with all this noise?"

I stuck my head out my bedroom door, just in time to see my mother struggling down the stairs with her typewriter.

"How do you expect *Laura* to concentrate?" she snarled. "How do you expect *Laura* to concentrate?" She squirmed through the "clients" who stood three deep all the way up the flight of steps. That is, some were standing. Others were sitting, sprawling or leaning. I hoped the banister wouldn't break.

"Gangway," she warned sullenly. "I said, *gangway,* dammit!"

Jamie and I exchanged nervous glances. I'd never seen my mother so surly before. Angry, yes. Upset, yes. But not like this.

"Sorry, Mrs. H," apologized Jamie. "Hope we didn't disturb you."

My mother, having reached the bottom of the stairs, turned to look up at us.

"Now what makes you think three hundred kids screaming in front of my door when I'm trying to write this damn book would *disturb me?*" She almost shrieked those last two words.

"And take that damn sign off the wall!" She charged out of sight.

A piece of paper was taped on the staircase wall. Someone—Douglas no doubt—had scrawled an arrow with Magic Marker and printed: "THIS WAY TO THE DOOM ROOM."

Jamie managed to work her way over to the sign and ripped it off the wall. She rolled her eyes at me. "Are you ready?"

"Yeah. Send the next one in."

I went back into my room and sat down on the bed. After a week and a half I had grown accustomed to the routine. In fact, I kind of enjoyed it.

The first day had been the worst. I was scared that nothing would happen. I was almost as scared that *something* would happen. But miraculously, I was able to see things for each of the five people Jamie brought to me. And none of the things I saw was that hard to figure out. Like, I saw a teacher hand Katie something, and Katie cried. So I knew she was going to fail English.

And I saw Barry Cohen in a big room, running back and forth in a pair of shorts, so I knew he'd make the basketball team. Things like that. There was only one really mysterious one the first day, and with that I did just what Jamie had told me to. I told Sue Ellen Priddy, whose reading it was, exactly what I had seen, and that I didn't know what it meant. She wasn't dissatisfied at all. In fact, although she was puzzled by what I told her, she was thrilled that I'd seen something, and swore she wouldn't rest till she figured out what it was.

And Jamie had been right. The more readings I gave, the easier it became and the faster I was able to "see" things. It was tiring, but not hard, if you know what I mean. And of course, the better I got, the more people marveled over my talent and the more confident I became. Now, a mere ten days after my first "client" I found that not only was I handling everything quite smoothly (with Jamie's help) but I had become very fond of all the fame and attention and popularity I'd suddenly attracted.

Not to mention the money. I'd decided to give half of it to charity and keep half for myself. Jamie had finally persuaded me to charge a fee and the sight of all that money piling up in my desk drawer helped to convince me she'd been right.

My family was exactly as unthrilled as I'd told

Jamie they would be. It was kind of strange. Here I'd gotten what I wanted most of all: an outstanding quality that would make me noticed even among my overachieving family and that would make my family notice me. Well, they noticed me, all right—but their reactions were not exactly those of wholehearted admiration and awe.

Douglas was furious. My mother seemed more and more worried every day. My father frowned and shook his head a lot. Jill thought it was okay, but the throngs made it too hectic around the house for her to rehearse, or memorize lines, or do her homework, or *anything*. In short, nobody said, "How lucky we are to have a gifted medium like Laura in the house!"

One problem was that the appointment scheme didn't work.

Even though Jamie started out by scheduling only eight appointments an afternoon, other kids came anyway, hoping to get "squeezed in." If we didn't let them in, they milled around the front lawn and refused to leave until they were sure the readings were over for the day. This made all our neighbors unthrilled.

There didn't seem to be anything we could do about it, so we declared Saturday afternoons "open" and I would just do as many readings as I could from one to five.

It cut down a little on the weekday traffic, but not enough to make a noticeable difference to my family. Jamie suggested extending the weekday hours from four to six, but I quickly vetoed that idea. I was having enough trouble trying to convince my parents and Douglas that after all, it was only for one hour a day, and if Destiny had chosen me to be a brilliant psychic, who was going to be foolhardy enough to thumb their nose at Destiny?

"Kool-Aid! Hey, anybody want Kool-Aid?"

I stuck my head out the door again.

Dennis walked carefully toward the stairs balancing a tray full of little paper cups. I closed my eyes, afraid to look.

"Steve Freeman," Jamie said to the boy in front of my door, "you're next. Go on in."

As I closed the door I could hear Dennis chanting, "Delicious, nutritious and good for you too. Ten cents a cup, drink it all up."

"Clever kid," Steve commented. I motioned him to the chair. He sat down and leaned forward eagerly.

"Yeah. Well." I pointed at the sign Jamie had put on my wall. It read: "THE MANAGEMENT ACCEPTS NO RESPONSIBILITY FOR *ANY-THING*. DONATION: $1.00."

"That's for legal reasons," Jamie said when I asked her about it. Since she seemed to be the authority on everything connected with the Prediction Business, I didn't question her any further.

"Now," I began, "you understand that I can't promise you that I can see into your future, that I might not see anything at all?"

Jamie and I had agreed that I had to be very

honest about my readings and explain all this in advance, so nobody could complain afterwards. There was no charge if I couldn't give a reading.

"Yeah, yeah, I know."

"And you know that whatever I tell you might not be right, that I'm not accurate one hundred percent of the time and there might be different ways of explaining what I see?"

"Right, right, I understand that too." Steve was very impatient to get started.

"Okay. Do you have a particular question you want me to try and answer, or do you just want a general reading?"

"No special question," Steve said. "Just tell me what you see in my future."

"Okey-doke." I sat back on the bed, propping myself against the wall with several throw pillows. I relaxed my body completely and closed my eyes. I concentrated on Steve's face, picturing it in my mind, not trying to force anything. Pretty soon —I guess it was pretty soon, because I'm never sure how long it actually takes—an image began to form.

At first it was all jumbled parts, but then pieces began to float together to make a whole, like a jigsaw puzzle being assembled under water.

It started with just a long, dimly-lit corridor, nothing more. After awhile I could see figures advancing. I couldn't see them clearly for quite some time. As if from a long distance, they slowly made their way toward me. It seemed like a line of people, a parade—maybe soldiers marching. No, not quite. They trudged down the corridor coming closer to me. It was almost as if I was standing right there, observing, although I was nowhere in the picture I was watching. Finally they came close enough to be seen clearly. There were six men, two of whom were carrying a long, flat object. What they were carrying was draped in a white sheet.

I came out of it with a little shudder.

Steve's eager face peered down at me. Only then did I remember I had been doing a reading for him. I stared, horrified at his lively, searching eyes. That was *his* body I had seen draped in a sheet. It must have been. Was it possible that he was going to die? Had that been his *funeral?*

"What is it? What did you see in my future?" Now he looked worried and no wonder. My face must have reflected the terror I felt.

I could barely get a word past my lips. "Nothing," I choked.

"You saw *something*. I know you did."

I shook my head. "Sick," I gasped. "I think I'm sick. Please."

"All right," he said doubtfully. "I hope you feel better. Should I put the dollar on the desk?"

"No, no! Just—no charge if I can't do it."

"Okay. Maybe next time." He let himself out of my room and I sank back against the pillows. My heart was pounding in my chest; I wondered briefly if I could be having a heart attack. It was horrible, terrifying. Steve was going to die and I knew it and he didn't. This was not at all the kind of future I expected to see into.

Jamie burst into my room and slammed the door.

"Laura, what's the matter? Steve said you were sick."

"No more readings today, Jamie. I can't."

"But we just *started*. We've got to—"

"No," I insisted. "No. I don't want to do any more today. I don't know if I ever want to do any more!"

"Why? Laura, what is it? What happened?"

"I saw Steve dead!" I shivered violently. I pulled myself to the edge of the bed and sat hunched over as I described the reading. Jamie sat down next to me and put her arm around my shoulders.

"Laura, take it easy. Don't you remember what I told you? Remember the giant bird and the football player? That doesn't necessarily mean that Steve is going to die. It could mean a whole lot of other things."

"Like what? What could that possibly mean?"

"Well, I don't know. That's just it. We can't tell yet. But there are lots of things it could be besides a funeral."

"You can't think of one other thing! I don't care, Jamie, I don't want to see things like that, whatever they mean. It's too scary."

"All right. Okay, why don't you take some time

to rest and have a nice cup of tea. Try to calm down and be reasonable. I'll hold them off for a while."

"Send them *home*. I'm not doing any more today."

"Laura, try and—"

There was a knock on my door.

"What is it?" Jamie called impatiently.

The door opened and a strange man stuck his head inside.

"Laura Hoffman?"

"I'm Laura Hoffman. What is it?"

He stepped into my room and closed the door.

"Lieutenant Cohen. Police." He flashed a wallet at me, which I guess contained his identification, but I was too startled to examine it.

"Police?" I echoed. "What do you—do you want *me?*"

Jamie stared at him and then at me, with complete bewilderment.

"You and my son are classmates," he said.

"Oh, you are Barry's father?" Jamie asked.

"That's right."

Thinking about my reading for Steve I was suddenly struck with an awful premonition of disaster.

"Barry!" I cried. "Is something wrong? What happened?"

"There is something wrong," he acknowledged.

"Oh, *no.*" I closed my eyes, afraid of what he was going to tell me had happened to Barry.

"Do you know that what you're doing is illegal?"

My eyes flew open.

"Illegal!" cried Jamie.

It took a moment to catch up with what was happening. I was so relieved to hear that Barry was okay that at first I didn't understand what his father was saying to me.

"That's right. Fortune-telling is against the law. You're taking money, aren't you?"

Jamie pointed to the sign. "Donations," she said. "Voluntary donations."

"Donations, love offerings, whatever you want to call it." Lieutenant Cohen shrugged. "It's money. That makes it illegal. I'm not with the Bunco Squad, but—"

"Bunco Squad!" I repeated.

"Yeah, you know, rackets, con games, swindles—"

Jamie was indignant. "This isn't a con game! Laura really is a psychic. What kind of a dumb law—"

"Look," he said patiently, "it may be a dumb law, but it *is* a law. As I say, I'm not with the Bunco Squad, but when Barry told me about the —what do you call it—reading?"

I nodded.

"The reading you gave him, I thought I'd come and see you. Unofficially, of course."

"Well, for heaven's sakes, if the police don't have anything better to do than—"

"Jamie!" I warned. There was no point in making a big fuss over this, because I'd been determined to go out of business anyway, at least temporarily. It was perfectly fine with me to be told I couldn't do any more readings.

"Thank you for warning me," I said to Lieutenant Cohen. "As a matter of fact, I was thinking of giving it up. But not because it was against the law. I mean, I had no idea it was against the law."

"I thought you might not know," he said. "Barry didn't either, and he was very upset when I told him. He was afraid you'd think he'd turned you in or something like that. I tried to explain to him I only wanted to protect a friend of his from getting into trouble. . . ."

"Well, thanks," I said. "I really mean it. It's just as well this happened."

"Barry made the basketball team, didn't he?" Jamie asked abruptly.

"Yes," Lieutenant Cohen replied. "Yes, he did." He looked at me for a moment, his eyes searching mine. I didn't want to lower my gaze. He might think I was a fraud or something if I couldn't look him straight in the eye.

Finally he said, "You really think you're psychic?"

"She doesn't *think* she's psychic," Jamie retorted. "She *is* psychic."

He shrugged, as if it really didn't matter one

way or the other. "Okay. Okay." He gave a little wave of his hand and left.

Jamie looked deflated. "It's a shame," she grumbled. "It's just a shame." She sighed. "I guess I'd better go and tell the kids to go home." She shook her head and mumbled something I didn't hear.

I followed her into the hall.

There had been an unusual hush, maybe because some of the kids recognized Barry's father, or maybe because Steve told them I was sick. But as soon as we came out, everyone started yelling questions at once.

Jamie finally succeeded in yelling "Quiet!" loud enough to have an effect. When she achieved this, she announced in a bitter voice, "We've been raided."

They began shouting again.

"I said shut up!" she screamed. "You will have to go home. Laura can't give any more readings or they'll throw her in the slammer."

At last she managed to convince them that there would be no more predictions today, and the disgruntled crowd began to disperse.

Douglas and Dennis stood in the front hall, watching everyone leave. Dennis looked positively doleful. Douglas was holding a big tray of something and stopping everyone he could grab before they got to the door.

The last person shook his head at Douglas and

left. Douglas looked up to where I stood at the top of the staircase.

"Drat," he said, with mock irritation. "And I just put up fourteen more hot dogs."

9

That week Mr. Kane called an extra rehearsal; the performance was only two weeks away. It was just as well that I couldn't give any more readings, because I had to stay late Monday, Wednesday and Thursday.

Not that we didn't know our parts. We did. In addition to our own parts, Beth and I and Jean Freeman knew practically the entire play by heart —everybody's parts. There was always a prompter in the wings with a full script, but most of the time if anyone had a minor attack of amnesia, Jean or Beth or I could cue her before the prompter.

Mr. Kane had postponed assigning understudies until rehearsals were well underway, because he didn't want anybody trying to learn two parts at once. He said it would be much easier to memorize the part you were going to understudy after you were completely sure of your own lines, and after you became familiar with the play.

I guess he also wanted to see who the fastest memorizers were, because he made Beth Jean's stand-in, and me, Beth's. It was perfectly logical to have Beth take Jean's role if she got sick, but I'm sure the only reason I understudied Beth was because I knew her lines perfectly. I couldn't *act* them, but I could say them in the right places.

"If you get sick, I'll kill you," I threatened Beth, when we found out about all this.

"And if Jean breaks a leg," Beth joked, "your prediction will come true. I could be the star after all."

"Don't say that!" I shuddered. "That means I'd have to take your part."

(To show you how vital my regular role of Nancy was, I had no understudy.)

Rita asked Mr. Kane why everyone didn't have a stand-in.

"Only the major roles have stand-ins."

(Not very much of an explanation, I thought.)

"And what if both Jean and Beth get sick?" asked Rita.

"They would not dare," he said grimly.

Every day that week the first thing I did when I got to school was to check Steve Freeman's desk. It was the first place my eyes rested as I entered homeroom. When he was there, I heaved a sigh of relief. The one day he came later than I did, I experienced such a wave of panic that Jamie had to practically hold my hand until he arrived. Once I knew he was safe I was able to relax until the next morning.

The following Monday I got to school later than usual. It had snowed during the night. Dennis had heard the weather forecast in the afternoon and had thoughtfully brought all the windshield deicer we had in the garage into the house, in case we were so snowbound that we couldn't get to the garage. It *was* considerate of him—and you can't really expect too much logic from a seven-year-old, so I don't think it was fair for Douglas to harp on the fact that if we couldn't get to the garage because of the snow, how did Dennis expect us to use the car at *all*, and if the car was in the garage overnight, why should it need the deicer?

As it turned out, we could get to the garage. It was ten degrees out at seven A.M. and it was a very icy walk up the driveway, but there was barely two inches of snow on the ground. The station wagon, however, wouldn't start, which meant that my father's car, left out all night in front of the house, *did* have to be deiced.

"See, you did need it!" Dennis told Douglas triumphantly.

The only thing was, Dennis could not remember exactly where he had put the three cans of deicer.

My mother insisted we all had to be driven to school or risk frostbite, as there were gale-force winds which made the wind-chill factor down around 20 below.

We looked everywhere Dennis thought he might have put the stuff until finally, exasperated, my father said to just get him a bottle of rubbing alcohol, it would do just as well. Only my mother couldn't find a bit of rubbing alcohol in the house, and she assumed that peroxide wouldn't work.

My father said, no, peroxide wouldn't work, it had to be alcohol, and did she want him to use the scotch or the bourbon to deice the windshield? She said neither one, because with the streets so icy if he skidded or something driving us to school or going to work and a cop came along and smelled the whole car reeking of scotch, there was bound to be a bit of trouble.

By this time Dennis had led us all over the house in search of the deicer, which he was certain he had put in an extremely safe place, if he could only recall what it was.

At that moment Jill remembered she had bowling that afternoon. She grabbed her bowling bag from the debris in the corner of the dining room. "There it is!" She pointed at three aerosol cans lined up in a neat little row.

"Oh, yeah," said Dennis brightly. "I remember. I put it behind Jill's bowling bag."

Which is why I got into school barely three minutes before first period bell.

The room was buzzing. Everyone seemed to be conferring with their neighbors, then turning to other people to compare what they'd heard. I had no idea what it was all about.

Jamie waved to me frantically as I hurried to my seat.

"Jean Freeman was in an accident yesterday," she told me, in an electrifying whisper. "And *Steve was too*. In the car."

I looked over toward Steve's seat, as if she might be wrong and he might actually be sitting right there, the same as usual. But he wasn't.

"The whole family," Jamie went on. "They were driving back from Connecticut and they were on the parkway, practically home, and they veered off the shoulder or something and there was this huge, seven-car pileup—"

"What happened to Steve?"

"He's okay. He's in the hospital but he's okay. They think he has a concussion."

"Thank God," I breathed. "At least he's not dead."

"No, he'll be okay. Jean is going to be in the hospital a while, though. She has internal injuries, whatever that is. They don't think it's too bad, but they can't be sure."

"It *sounds* bad," I said, shaken. "How did you find out?"

"The principal said it on the PA before you got here. He said Jean was at Southside General if anyone wanted to send cards or call or anything."

123

"What about the parents?"

"He didn't say. I guess they're all right. I really don't know."

The first period bell rang. Reluctantly I got up to walk to the door. I wanted to find out more, as much as I could, about the accident and I really felt too stunned to sit through Science just then.

Jamie yanked at my sleeve. "I was thinking," she whispered, following me out the door, "about what you saw in Steve's reading, and you know what? That must have been a stretcher, not a coffin. And they must have been carrying him on the stretcher to a hospital room. That would explain everything."

It made sense. The only part that wasn't right was the sheet pulled up over his face, but I didn't think it had to be *exact*. After all, Jamie didn't really have a mark on her temple, either. It was just something you had to figure out.

"I'll bet you're right," I agreed. "That must have been what I saw."

"It's terrible about Jean," she said as we scrambled down the hall, "but I can't help thinking what a terrific psychic you are."

Halfway through Science it hit me.

Beth was Jean's stand-in.

Beth *was* going to be the star of the play.

Everything I had predicted was coming true.

Beth was waiting outside Mr. Kane's room before our English class started. When she spotted me coming down the hall she ran to meet me, jostling her way through the stream of kids moving in the opposite direction.

"Laura, I can't believe it! Isn't that the most awful thing about Jean? Remember when I said that about her breaking a leg, and then I'd be the star of the play and your prediction would come true after all? Oh, Laura, it was a *joke*. I never meant I really wanted anything to happen to Jean—"

I stopped dead in the middle of the hallway, oblivious to the onrushing students shoving past me on all sides. Why had it taken me so long to realize? All through first period I had been so preoccupied with the terrible news of the accident, and the way in which my predictions had come true, that I had failed to give the least bit of thought to what *else* would result from all this.

And now the rest of it hit me, like that old ton of bricks.

Beth was Jean's understudy.

I was Beth's understudy.

I would have to do the second biggest part in the play.

"Mr. Kane!" Beth stopped him at the door. "What are we going to do? Did you hear about Jean?"

The look of distress on his face made it plain that he had.

"We'll meet this afternoon," he said. "I'll have an announcement on the PA during homeroom."

"I *can't*," Beth wailed. "I have an orchestra rehearsal this afternoon."

"You'll have to get out of it," he said sharply. "If the show does go on, we can't very well do it without Eloise."

I couldn't play Beth's part. I just couldn't. I would be awful. You can't have a rotten actress in the second lead of a play; I would ruin the whole thing. Even if I were not too scared to open my mouth and say my lines, the simple truth was I could not act. I was not Jill. I was not Beth. I was Laura.

And I was scared to death.

Beth was late to lunch because she had to see Mr. Schwartz about missing the rehearsal. She was convinced she'd be tossed out of the orchestra on her ear, but when she got into the lunchroom and settled into the seat I'd saved for her, she was relieved.

"He was annoyed," she reported, "but I explained what the problem was and that after this week I wouldn't miss practice no matter what. Our concert is only a week from Friday—at least I'm not a soloist or anything."

I nodded, not really able to worry too much about Beth's scheduling conflicts. She went to get her lunch. By the time she returned I had finished mine, and was staring blankly off into space, not seeing anything at all.

"Do you think we're going to do the play anyway?" she asked.

I just shrugged. How could I say, "I hope not," when I knew she must think this was her big chance?

She dug into a small mound of chow mein. "What's the matter with you? You're so quiet."

I turned to look at her. "Don't you realize what this means?"

"What what means? The play?"

"Yes, the play. If you're Eloise, who do you think will play Phyllis?"

"You, of course." Unconcerned, she sipped at her milk.

"And that doesn't worry you?"

"Why should it?"

"Because I'll be awful! Don't you care that I'll ruin the play you're the star of?"

She smiled. "Sure I'd worry if I thought you'd ruin the play. But you won't. You're nowhere near as untalented as you think. You just never had a chance to do a good part."

"Oh, *Beth*. You're a very loyal friend and I know you don't want to hurt my feelings, but I know perfectly well how un-talented I am. I wanted a little, teeny part. The more we rehearsed, the gladder I was I *had* a little, teeny part, and now this has to happen."

"Wait and *see* what happens," Beth said. "We're not even sure yet whether we'll do the play. If we do, I'll rehearse with you every day this week and we'll help each other. It's a new part for me too, you know."

"Oh, sure," I retorted, "but it's the part you wanted. I never wanted to be Phyllis."

"You'll rise to the occasion," Beth assured me. "Some are born to greatness and others have greatness thrust upon them. That's a famous quotation," she added.

"I'm not ready for greatness!"

Beth shrugged. "That's the whole point. Greatness doesn't always ask if you're ready."

10

The cast of the play met in Mr. Kane's room since the orchestra had the auditorium for that afternoon. The situation was discussed and all the pros and cons were weighed. There were about twelve variations on the theme "The show must go on."

I thought I would scream if I heard one more "The show must go on."

Why must the show go on?

"We've worked so hard."

"So many people will be disappointed."

(Not me.)

"We owe it to the audience."

(What audience?)

Finally we took a vote. "All those in favor of doing the play as scheduled, with the understudies, raise their hands." I was surrounded by a forest of waving arms.

"All those opposed."

Every tree in the forest fell. Frankly, I was too chicken to raise my hand to cast the only "No" vote, so I just looked around with pretended nonchalance, as if checking the votes. I hoped no one would notice I hadn't voted.

We moved all the desks to one side of the room clearing an area to serve as a stage. Mr. Kane said we would just do a run-through of the play today, to make sure the understudies knew their new parts.

Rita, who hadn't been in the cast, was given my old part of Nancy, so there wouldn't have to be any more shifting of roles. She had to use a script for the rehearsal, but she was sure she'd have the lines memorized in no time. It was hardly a demanding role.

As well as Beth and I knew the play, we stumbled over a few lines, mostly because we forgot what our cues were. I went through the whole rehearsal practically numb with fear; I kept thinking about doing this on a stage, in front of an audience. That made it hard to keep my mind on rehearsing.

Even though it was only supposed to be a walkthrough, Mr. Kane made suggestions. Especially to me.

"You look a little stiff, Phyllis. Try and relax."
Hah!

"Put the stress on 'were,' not 'you.' 'You *were* the best team.'"

"Phyllis, don't stop talking before Nancy interrupts you. And Nancy, be sure and cut in before she finishes her line. Start your line just before Phyllis says, 'think.'"

By the time we were done, I was exhausted. It was the strain of learning to do a new part, and the nervousness that didn't get better but worse as I realized that even though I knew the lines pretty well, I didn't know Phyllis's movements and was not at all sure of where I was supposed to stand or move to, or what I was supposed to pick up or put down.

"That wasn't bad," Mr. Kane said. "We'll have the stage tomorrow and that will make things a lot easier for you. Eloise and Phyllis, you'd better work on your cues a bit tonight. You're not entirely sure of them."

Beth and I walked to my house together. It was still bitter cold and icy, but the weather was the least of my worries.

"You were fine," Beth insisted. "It was only a walk-through."

"What walk-through?" I said sarcastically. "I was *acting*. Couldn't you tell?"

"We'll work on it tonight. We can really help each other out. And if Jill is home I'll bet she'll give us some tips."

"You don't need any tips," I said.

"I sure need practice, though." Beth actually sounded a little worried.

Douglas was at the piano as we let ourselves into the house. We went straight into the kitchen, where my parents and Jill greeted us as if we had hitchhiked down from the North Pole.

"You must be frozen!" my mother cried. "Why didn't you call? We could have picked you up. I'll make some cocoa."

Dennis was under the kitchen table with a swarm of Matchbox cars.

"Hi, Beth. Want to see my traffic jam?"

Beth looked down. "It's a pretty good traffic jam," she said.

"It's the best one I ever did. Everybody crashes up."

"Which reminds me," I began. "Wait'll you hear this."

"*Dammit dammit dammit!*" Dennis piped. "You stupid Sunday driver. Dammit yourself, meathead!"

My mother rolled her eyes. "Ignore him," she mouthed at us.

"That won't be easy," I sighed, as Dennis erupted with a long string of curses.

"He really must meet by brother," whispered Beth. "Roger would love him."

"It's a p-h-a-s-e," Jill told her. "It just started fifteen minutes ago, out of the clear blue sky."

My mother placed the cocoa cups on the table. "We're hoping for the shortest phase in history."

My father interrupted Dennis's next stream of choice words by asking, "How about a game of Go Fish, Den?"

"That's great psychology," muttered Jill, "rewarding the kid for having a dirty mouth."

Dennis emerged from under the table. "Yeah," he said eagerly.

They went off in search of the cards.

"It's called distraction," my mother told Jill. "Which is what he will drive me to," she added.

"Do you think," I said, my voice cold, "that I might get a few words in edgewise now?"

"I'm sorry, dear. What is it? What's happened?"

Beth and I told them about the accident, and the play, and how I would have to replace Beth in the second lead.

Jill's first reaction was, "Laura was right! Beth *is* going to be the star!"

"I was right about more than that," I said casually.

Then I had to explain to them about the reading I'd done on Steve, because they had never heard about it before. Now that I knew he was going to be all right, I got a certain amount of satisfaction in telling them of my prediction and seeing expressions of amazement.

At first Beth was a little annoyed that I hadn't told her when Jamie had known all about it. My mother kept gazing at me, shaking her head and saying, "How incredible—it's awful—to think you predicted that!"

"At least," said Jill, "this will finally give Laura the chance to find out she's not such a bad actress."

"Will you help us?" asked Beth. "We really could use some coaching."

" 'We' meaning me." I said, "not her."

" 'We' meaning both of us," Beth corrected.

"Of course, I'll be glad to." Jill looked as if she'd enjoy it. "Give me a copy of the script and let me read it first."

Beth pulled her battered script out of her loose-leaf and gave it to Jill, who went off to her room to go over it. Beth and I started setting the table. Dinner would be in a little while, since it was already pretty late.

I was placing the forks beside the napkins when suddenly the china and silver disappeared and in their place I saw a photograph album. I don't think I stopped to realize I was having another vision; I was just into it, before I knew what was happening.

My mother was turning the pages of the album very slowly. There seemed to be only one picture on each of the black pages. They looked like old-fashioned portraits, with oval frames around the faces.

A page turned, and there was a picture of Douglas. Underneath the picture, in old-fashioned, flowery script, was written "Douglas."

Another page turned. I saw a photo of Jill, with her name beneath in the same handwriting.

My mother turned the page again. There I was, looking out from the oval frame, my name on the page like the others.

Very slowly now the last page was turned. "Dennis" was written under the photograph, just as all the other names had been. But in the oval frame, where Dennis's face should be, there was nothing but a blank, white space.

"Laura!" Beth was shaking my shoulder. Confused, I looked around. I was in the kitchen and I was standing there with a bunch of silverware in my hand. My mother was staring at me.

"What was it, Laura?" Beth demanded. "Did you see something?"

I was scared again, just as I had been the first time I had seen my mother with the dolls. The silver began to clank in my hand, which suddenly felt shaky. I hastily resumed setting the table to cover up my fright. My mother's anxious face was enough to persuade me not to tell her what I had seen.

"No, I was just daydreaming," I replied finally, to Beth's repeated questions.

"Are you sure?" asked my mother.

"Yeah, I'm sure."

"Well, all right. But you looked so . . ."

"You really did," Beth agreed.

"I'm *starved*," I announced loudly. "Aren't you, Beth? When do we eat?"

"About five minutes," my mother replied. Beth gave me a funny look, as if she saw right through my attempt to change the subject, but my mother was stirring something on the stove and her back was to me. If she thought I sounded a little unnatural, she didn't press it.

"I'll go tell Jill. Come on, Beth."

Beth followed me up the stairs.

"You did see something," she whispered. "I knew it."

"Wait till we get Jill," I said. "I'll tell you about it."

We knocked on Jill's door and went into her room. She was sprawled out on the bed, script in her hand.

"This isn't a bad play. Shakespeare it isn't, but for Junior High it could be worse."

"Listen, Jill, we're going to eat in five minutes and I have to make this quick. I want to tell you about something."

First I told her about my mother and the three dolls. Beth waited patiently till I was finished, though I knew she was dying to hear what the latest was.

"Now, just a minute ago I had another. See if this doesn't sound like it means practically the same thing to you."

I told them about the photograph album and the empty frame.

Jill looked shaken. Beth nodded slowly as if she could see the connection between the two episodes.

"What do you think?" I asked.

"I don't know," Jill replied. "Did you tell Mom about this?"

"No. I was afraid it would worry her."

"It sure would. It worries me. Whatever it means, Laura, it can't be good. I'm really frightened."

"Yeah, me too. I'm going to keep waiting for something to happen and I don't know what it is."

"I know. But it has to mean something is going to happen to Dennis."

"Not necessarily something bad." Beth tried to sound comforting.

"That's what Jamie said," I added, "but still . . ."

Jill sighed heavily and pulled herself off the bed.

"Maybe not." But you could tell she didn't believe that for an instant. Neither did I, not anymore. And neither did Beth.

Jill helped us read through the play after dinner, but our hearts weren't in it. We kept stopping to go over my predictions again, to try and make something less frightening out of them.

Finally Jill said, "Look, we're not helping anyone this way. Let's concentrate on the play. We'll just keep an eye on Dennis from now on and that's all we can do."

"Maybe you ought to tell your mother," said Beth. "She's the one who's with him most of the time. Maybe she ought to know so she can be extra careful."

"But if it's a prediction," Jill argued, "and it's going to happen, there's nothing she can do to prevent it. What's the use of giving her even more grief before it happens?"

We didn't have any answers for that.

"Remember how you felt when you thought Steve was going to die? You just got finished telling us how you were a nervous wreck all that week from worrying about him. Do you want Mom to go through that?"

"No, but—"

"Besides, she can't stay with him in school every day, so for most of the time she's not with him anyway. I don't see that it would do any good to tell her. We'll just do the best we can at watching him and leave it at that. In the meanwhile, you people have a play to rehearse."

11

Jill was a big help to us. (Me, really. Just as I thought, Beth didn't need much help at all.) She worked with us for the next two evenings after our regular rehearsals, showing me how to move more naturally and how to "get into" the part of Phyllis, rather than just reciting her lines.

"See, you're really very capable of doing this part," she told me on Wednesday night, when I was acting better than I'd ever dreamed I could. "All you needed was a little coaching. And everyone needs that."

When we were home, Jill and I watched Dennis like hawks. Fortunately, she was able to get in right after school on Tuesday and Wednesday and she could look out on the yard from her bedroom window. At night it was no problem, because we just made sure we knew where he was in the house. If he wasn't underfoot, he was usually watching television.

Friday afternoon we had the dress rehearsal. We were to do the play exactly as we were going to present it that night. There were three changes of costume we had to make. For one midnight scene we had to be in pajamas and nightshirts, for the last scene we had to be in shorts and T-shirts dyed to match (our basketball team uniforms) and the rest of the time we wore regular jeans or skirts and shirts. We had a big room right next to the stage entrance to change in, with a sheet pinned over the glass in the door so no one could see in.

A couple of the costume changes between scenes had to be made really fast, which made me very anxious about getting back onstage in time for my cues, but the clothes were really so simple that it was easier than I thought it would be.

On the other hand, I was not very good at dress rehearsal.

I missed a couple of lines and that shook me up so that I began to think of how awful it would be if I forgot my lines during the performance. Once I began to think about that, I was too scared to remember how well I'd been doing with Jill's coaching and forgot almost everything she'd told me.

Mr. Kane tried to maintain a cheerful air, insisting we'd all be fine and the play would be a smash.

He kept repeating that old saying about how a bad dress rehearsal means a good performance. But every once in a while I caught him with a wistful expression on his face and I was sure he was thinking, If only Jean were here.

We'd sent her a big bunch of flowers from the whole club. Steve was back in school, and the parents were okay except for some bruises and cracked ribs. Jean was going to be laid up at least another week.

I got home at five. We were supposed to be back in school by seven. Beth's parents had invited us over after the play for coffee and cake. Dennis could meet Roger and her parents would meet mine.

Dennis and Douglas were playing blackjack for money at one corner of the dining room table, so Dennis was obviously still okay.

I reported the Traubs' invitation to my mother after she asked me how the rehearsal had gone, and she said that would be nice. Douglas said, "I don't have to go, do I?"

"You don't want to?" asked my mother.

"Nah. What for?"

"What for indeed?" she repeated. "I guess we can manage without you."

I couldn't eat a thing at dinner. I was absolutely certain that if I put one morsel of food in my mouth I'd throw up. All the butterflies in the world were holding their annual convention in my stomach.

"At least have some toast and tea," my mother urged. "You'll feel much worse if you don't eat at all."

"I couldn't feel worse."

"You'll be more alert and you'll give a better performance if you have a little something in you," she insisted.

"It's true," Jill agreed.

"I won't give a good performance no matter what I eat."

"Oh, yes you will," said Jill. "You'll be nervous till you speak your first couple of lines and then you'll be great. You'll forget all about your stage fright."

"I'll be lucky if I don't forget my first couple of lines," I groaned.

"You *have* to have a little toast," my mother kept on.

"All right, all right!" I cried. "Stop nagging me. I'll have a piece of toast."

My father patted my hand and smiled his encouragement.

Dennis said, "You're going to be the star of the play, right, Laura? And I can stay up late, right? *Very* late? And wear my bow tie. And my pith helmet."

"Dear, I know you don't believe this now, but by next week you'll look back on this and wonder what you were so worried about." My mother put two pieces of buttered toast in front of me.

"You're assuming," I croaked, "that I live through tonight."

"I guarantee it," she grinned. "Did I ever tell you about *The Sons of Diego Cortez*"?

My father glanced toward the ceiling, closed his eyes and murmured, "Good heavens."

"Everyone knew," she began, "that we were making the biggest bomb since *Slaves of the Invisible Monster*. The script was by the producer's fourteen-year-old son, with additional dialogue by a chimpanzee who enjoyed playing with a typewriter."

"But you were very good," my father said loyally.

"Thank you, darling." She turned back to me. "I was utterly dreadful. Appalling. My lines consisted of gems like 'Hey, gringo, you lookin' for Cortez?' The whole movie was on that exalted level. We went through the film with a sense of impending doom, and by the time it was over we were all so depressed we nearly made a mass suicide pact. The day the movie opened we hid, which wasn't necessary because nobody took any notice of the film at all. We got one review and the movie played for two days somewhere and disappeared into oblivion."

"What did the review say?" Jill asked. "Did it mention you?"

"No, thank God. It was one line long. It said, '*The Sons of Diego Cortez*: It would have been a mercy had they died in infancy.'"

Douglas groaned. "That's lousy, all right."

"But I lived through it," my mother emphasized. "We all did. And I'm *laughing* about it now. And your play isn't a turkey. And you won't be half as awful as I was in that. You couldn't be."

"At least *everyone* was awful in your movie," I said. "That's a lot better than being the only one who stinks."

I managed to get down—and keep down—a piece of toast and a cup of tea. Jill suggested that I go up and rest awhile. Since Douglas had begun to play the piano and Dennis was explaining to my mother that he couldn't wipe up the milk with *her* paper towels because Bounty was the quicker picker-upper and she ought to take it from Rosie, I decided that some time alone in my room might be a very good idea.

I stretched out on my bed.

Calm, Laura, calm, I told myself. Relax. Everything's going to be fine. Relax, toes. Relax, feet. I wiggled my toes and willed them to relax. I was going to work the tension out of my whole body, starting with my feet and moving all the way up to my head. I had read somewhere that that was as good as a tranquilizer.

But some place between my toes and my knees I lost track of my relaxing exercise, and my room faded away as if swallowed up by fog. The next thing I saw was a big door with a glass window in it, very much like the door of the room we were using next to the stage to change in. As the fog swirled away a huge silver star appeared on the window. It gleamed and shot rays of light out from its five points, almost as if it were an enormous diamond.

A girl with dark hair was walking toward it, her back to me. She looked up at the star and opened the door to go into the room. She turned around to face me—although of course, I wasn't actually there—and stood in the doorway, a big, contented smile on her face.

An now that I could see her face—

I was back in my room. A great feeling of serenity came over me, dissolving the tenseness of just a few moments ago. I'd recognized the girl in the doorway.

She was me.

Suddenly I was sure everything was going to be all right. I was sure that the vision meant that I could relax now, because I was going to do well in the play.

I didn't think it necessarily meant I would be a star, but that it was just sort of a sign that nothing would go wrong.

I got up from my bed and went over to my mirror to brush my hair. It would be time to leave for school pretty soon.

I was ready.

12

"Are there a lot of people out there?" Beth asked.

Rita, who'd peeked through the edge of the curtain from the wings, just nodded. She looked too scared to trust her voice.

Even Beth was a little pale.

I was nervous too, but not the same way as before. Now I felt a sort of scary anticipation, wishing that we would get started and dreading it at the same time. But I didn't feel paralyzed with fear, and I wasn't convinced that I'd forget all my lines and ruin the play. I just had a normal, average case of stage fright.

"Places everybody," said Mr. Kane.

Someone—Rita, I think—gave a little shriek of terror and we scrambled onstage to take our places for the first act.

There was a brief wait—though it certainly didn't seem brief as I stood there, trembling—while the principal gave us the standard introduction. Then Mr. Kane whispered, "Curtain," and the audience applauded as the curtain was raised and Act One began.

I was the first person in the play to speak. Not only that, I had to walk across stage to answer a telephone. My knees shook as the phone rang. I couldn't see too well past the footlights, not individual faces or anything, but I could see that there was a whole auditorium full of people gazing at me.

I picked up the receiver.

"Sigma Phi house." My voice squeaked a little and it didn't come out loud enough. So I took a deep breath and repeated it, remembering to *project,* so they could hear me in any part of the auditorium.

"Sigma Phi house. What can I do for you? Within reason, of course."

That got a responsive chuckle from the audience.

I could make them laugh! I *did* make them laugh. I was communicating with those people on the other side of the footlights.

I turned partially around to face them and went on with my lines.

"Hello? *Hello?* Is anyone there?" I waited a moment, as I was supposed to. "Is this a crank call? Did you spend a dime just to breathe at me?" I waited another moment. "Is anyone there?" I repeated loudly. I shrugged, looking toward the other girls on stage with me. "Well, it's been grand talking to you. We must do this again some time."

I hung up the phone as the audience laughed. What a strange feeling it was. What an unfamiliar sensation of power and confidence!

Jill was right. I felt fine now.

Everything went perfectly. We made our changes in time, the lighting cues came at exactly the right moments, no one forgot her lines. When the final curtain came down, there were loud cheers mixed in with the applause, mostly from kids in school who had come and from the brothers and sisters of cast members.

We were so exhilarated we jumped around behind the curtain hugging each other and squealing.

Mr. Kane put a stop to that immediately.

"Girls! Curtain call!"

We hastily assembled ourselves into a straight line and clasped hands as we'd practiced. The curtain went up. As the applause continued we bent down in a bow that we were supposed to make all together, but which turned out a bit ragged.

The applause increased and Mr. Kane said, "Phyllis and Eloise."

Beth and I stepped forward two paces in front of the rest of the cast and bowed. I'd never felt so special in my life. All those people were clapping for *me*. Because they thought I was a good actress. I clutched Beth's hand tightly, so happy I thought I would burst with it. We stepped back.

They were still applauding, almost as loudly.

"Eloise," hissed Mr. Kane.

Beth came forward and took a deep bow by herself. I clapped wildly, along with the rest of the audience.

The curtain was lowered.

We were all babbling at once now and there was no stopping us.

"You were wonderful!" Beth said. She hopped around the stage, yanking me along with her. "I knew it! I knew you could do it!"

"You were the wonderful one," I said, bouncing around, bumping into people. "And you were great," I said to Sonia, "and you were great," I said to Rita Lovett—of all people. I threw my arms out wide. "We were *all* great!"

Mr. Kane herded us offstage into the dressing room.

"You were great, girls," he said proudly.

"See, I told you," I giggled.

"Everything was perfect. The audience loved you. Congratulations on a fine performance."

We cheered and applauded ourselves.

"Oh, Mr. Kane," Rita cried, "I never knew doing a play was so neat! When do we do the next one?"

Mr. Kane's shoulders sagged. He rubbed his eyebrows with his fingers. For the first time I noticed how exhausted he looked.

"You'd better change now," he said weakly, letting himself out the door. "Your parents will be waiting to congratulate you."

"I'll bet," I told Beth, "he's going to make a run for the nearest bar."

We gathered our costumes together. We were still so excited that we continued to jabber away at each other as we thundered down the hall like stampeding cattle.

"You were marvelous!" my mother cried, hugging me to her.

Beth had gone to locate her parents and my family clustered around me, making quite a fuss about my performance.

"This is the girl," Jill declared, "who said she couldn't act."

"You really weren't bad," Douglas admitted. "I was surprised, no kidding. I really was surprised."

"I knew she could do it," my father said proudly. "Wasn't bad," he snorted. He glared at Douglas. "She was *excellent*."

"Oh, come on," I said, feeling a little embarrassed by all the lavish praise. "I wasn't that great. But I wasn't as bad as I thought I'd be. Was I?"

"I saw you right away," Dennis said. "You were the first one. I waved, but you didn't wave back."

"I didn't see you. Did you like the play?"

"Yeah. It was scary. You know what time it is? It's *late*. Do I have to go to bed now? Are we going right home?"

"We're going to Beth's house first," my mother said. "Don't you remember? You're going to meet her little brother."

Beth came charging down the hall, dragging her parents along. Roger lagged behind them, looking sullen.

Beth's parents were wearing their coats, so I couldn't see the rest of their clothes. I glanced hastily at my father and mother to see if they looked respectable. My mother had left the mink at home and my father had not put his Russian astrakhan cap back on yet, so they both seemed presentable enough. Somehow they had managed to convince Dennis that the occasion was not formal enough for his pith helmet, although he was wearing his bow tie.

"Wasn't Laura wonderful?" Beth's mother said warmly.

"Oh, we thought Beth was superb," my mother responded. "She has real talent."

"And to think," Mr. Traub said with a grin that

displayed his dazzling teeth, "just two days ago, before she was famous, this budding star was setting our table." He pulled a strand of my hair playfully.

I glowed.

"Well, why don't we get going?" Mrs. Traub suggested.

"Do you want to follow my car?" Beth's father asked, "or should I just give you the directions and we'll meet at the house?"

My father took the directions and we all trooped out to the parking lot. We planned to drop Jill and Douglas at home and then go on to the Traubs'.

"They seem like nice people," my father commented as we slowly joined the line of cars jockeying for position at the exits.

"*He* is incredible," Jill murmured. "I can't believe he's somebody's parent."

"You wouldn't," my father said, sounding almost jealous, "trade your poor old father in for that flashy new model, would you?"

"Of course not," Jill comforted him. "But if he wanted to trade his poor old wife in for *me* . . ."

We had cake and cocoa and coffee at the Traubs'. Beth and I huddled in her room reliving the play while our parents lingered over coffee. Roger and Dennis hit it off right away, which surprised me since they weren't that much alike. However they disappeared into the den together to watch reruns of "The Untouchables," which was usually on too late for them to see, so that might have been part of the reason for their compatibility.

It was a short visit. We left after about an hour and a half with our parents promising to get together again soon.

"You'll have to come and see us," my mother urged.

I cringed at the thought of the Traubs' first glimpse of us in our Natural Habitat, but what could you do? Etiquette is etiquette and surely my mother would ask them on a Friday or Saturday night, right after the maid had come to shovel the house.

"Very nice people," my father repeated as we drove home.

"Yes," my mother agreed. She glanced over at Dennis, who was practically asleep in the back seat. "She's very sweet. But don't you think he's a little—you know—plastic?"

"Plastic!" I howled. "How can you say that? You don't even know him! He's *super*."

"Shh! I'm sorry, I'm sorry. It was just sort of a first impression I got of him. You know him better, so you're probably right. He probably *is* super.

"He certainly is," I muttered.

My parents exchanged one of those knowing glances that usually make me furious. But by now I was too exhausted to argue any further.

It was silly to argue, anyhow. My whole family was proud of me, Mr. Traub had called me a star, Dennis was perfectly okay, and I was psychic.

Everything was wonderful.

13

I knocked at my mother's door. "Come," she said briskly.

"Where is everyone?" I asked. "It's so quiet around here."

"I know." She smiled like a contented cat. "Isn't it lovely? At this very moment, Linnet is on the threshold of the sealed room, just about to discover the hideous truth about the first Mrs. Glengariff."

"What *is* the hideous truth?"

"I wish I knew," she sighed. She leaned back in her chair. "But don't worry—I'll come up with something horrible any minute now."

"I'm sure you will. But where are all the people who are supposed to be *here?*"

"Let's see." She tapped her pencil thoughtfully

against her cheek. "Jill had something or other she had to stay for this afternoon. At least, I think it was this afternoon. And Douglas went over to Al's house—or the Chesters' maybe. Well, one or the other. They're forming a jazz quartet—did you ever hear of a quartet with piano, guitar, tuba and piccolo?"

She was in one of her vague moods. I felt my apprehension build as she spoke. She didn't really know where *anyone* was—she'd been off on the coast of Cornwall dreaming up hideous secrets all afternoon.

"Actually, I think the piccolo player is some girl they're all trying to impress, and they just asked her to be in the group so they could get to know her bet—"

"Where's Dennis?"

"He's downstairs, watching television."

"No, he's not!"

"Well, that's where I told him to stay until it was time for me to drive him to Roger's."

"Well he's not there now!" My voice was shrill. She couldn't understand why I was so upset.

"Then he must have gone outside."

"No, he's not. He's not out front, he's not in the backyard. I haven't seen him anywhere on the block and I looked all over the house for him."

"But where would he have gone? He was dying to go to Roger's and I told him just to wait fifteen minutes—"

"When did you tell him that?"

"About three-fifteen."

"It's four-thirty now!" I cried.

She leaped out of her chair. "It can't be! What happened to—I completely lost track of the time."

"Not to mention your kid," I muttered.

"Maybe he went to Stevie's," she said. She grabbed the phone. "Or to the Brills'. You call them on Jill's phone, I'll call the Elmans."

He wasn't with Stevie Elman or Larry Brill. They hadn't seen him since they came home from school.

"He's got to be *somewhere*," my mother insisted. "Did you look in the basement?"

"I just yelled, I didn't look. I'll go look now."

But even as I went down the basement steps, I knew he wouldn't be there. He was gone, like the picture and the doll. And it wasn't really my mother's fault. If I'd told her, she wouldn't have let him out of her sight. *Why hadn't I told her?* I knew she wasn't the kind of mother to hover over her children every second of the day. But Dennis was never the kind of kid to just take off on his own either. He liked to be with people and most of the time if he wasn't watching television or counting, he was with one or the other of us. I should have told her though. Even if it had made her worry; a little worry would have been better than this. It might even have prevented it.

He was not in the basement.

"I called the Traubs," she said. "I thought he

might have decided to go on his own. He's not there."

"Oh, Mom, he doesn't know how to get there. Besides, it's all the way across town. He couldn't possibly walk."

Jill came in just then.

"Dennis is missing," I said.

She dropped her books on the bed. "When? How do you know he's missing?"

"He's not here," I said simply.

"Look, Jill, you and Laura go up this block and down Laurel Crescent and Larch and yell for him. I'll take the car and go around the neighborhood. He probably just went for a walk. *Go on.*"

She ran downstairs. A moment later the front door slammed.

Jill looked at me, her face pale. "We knew it was going to happen. We should have been more careful. How long has he been gone?"

"We're not sure. She hasn't seen him since three-fifteen."

"Has she called the police?"

"I don't think so. He really hasn't been missing so very long."

"We'd better get going. You take this block and Larch and I'll go up Laurel and Beechwood."

Outside, we went our separate ways. I started up the street yelling, "Dennis!" every five seconds. Mrs. Brill stuck her head out the front door when she heard me calling.

"Didn't find him yet?"

I thought that was pretty obvious, since if we had found him I wouldn't be walking the streets yelling for him. I shook my head.

"Don't worry. He'll turn up."

She closed the door and I resumed the search. He wasn't on our block, or if he was, he didn't hear me. I started down Larch. I yelled his name in front of every house, thinking he might be inside visiting somewhere. I went around the sides of houses and looked in backyards, but no Dennis.

When I got back home, Jill and my mother were already there. Their faces fell when they saw I was alone.

"Did you call Dad?" I asked.

"No. He should be home any minute anyway. No point in worrying him." Jill and I exchanged guilty glances at that familiar phrase.

"What about the police?" asked Jill. "Shouldn't we call them? They cover more territory than we can."

"Yes, I think I'd better," my mother said. "At least they can be on the lookout for him, though I don't think he's officially missing until he's been gone overnight."

She bit her lip and quickly turned away from us.

By seven o'clock there was still no word of Dennis. My father and Douglas had come home and we had sent out for a couple of pizzas which nobody could eat. Beth called every half-hour to find out if Dennis had gotten home and to report that he hadn't shown up at her house.

My mother kept phoning the police to find out if they had any news yet. They repeated that as soon as they had anything they'd call her.

Finally they promised to send someone out to the house, probably just to get her off their backs. Since they had a complete description of Dennis already, I couldn't see the point of a personal visit, but it seemed to relieve my parents a little.

"At least they're doing something," my mother said. "At last."

At seven-thirty the doorbell rang. Jill and Douglas raced to the door and flung it open.

"I'm Lieutenant Cohen." The man in the gray suit spotted me behind Douglas. "Hi there. I recognized the address. Thought I'd come over and see if I could be of some help."

"He's the father of a boy in my class," I explained, when my parents looked questioningly in my direction.

"Is there any news?" asked my mother.

"Nothing yet, I'm afraid. But you know, he really hasn't been gone that long. Even though he's only seven, we don't consider him a missing person yet."

"He's never gone off like this before," my father said. "He's the kind of a child who stays quite close to home."

"Well, this usually happens once during childhood, at least," said Lieutenant Cohen, "even with the most dependable kids. Was he angry or upset about anything? Had he been punished? Was there any reason he might have run away from home?"

My mother looked embarrassed. "I'd promised to take him over to a friend's house," she said. "Then I lost track of the time and the next thing I knew it was four-thirty and he was gone."

"Did you call the friend?"

"Oh, yes. We've been in touch ever since he was missing. He never showed up there. It's way over in Country Manor. He wouldn't know how to begin to get there."

"Let's get a description of the boy and what he was wearing," the lieutenant said.

"But you have that already," my mother objected. "I gave them all the information on the phone."

"Let's go over it again," he insisted. "You might remember something else."

Douglas scowled. As my father and mother led Lieutenant Cohen into the living room he whispered, "Just busywork—to make it look like they're doing something when they're not."

Jill nodded despondently. "You're probably right," she said, "but what else is there to do?"

"Blue corduroy pants, red plaid flannel shirt. His winter jacket, navy blue with a hood. It's fake fur, nylon plush, I think. Forty-five inches tall. About forty-five pounds. He recites commercials by heart."

Lieutenant Cohen wrote everything down in a

little black notebook, although he must have had all that information already.

"Any relatives or grandparents he might have gone to visit?"

"Not around here," my father replied. "There's no one nearby."

My mother started to cry.

"Now, Mrs. Hoffman," Lieutenant Cohen said, "it's too soon to get that upset. This is your first experience with this kind of thing, but believe me, it happens every day. He'll turn up pretty soon. Most of them do."

"*Most* of them!" my mother repeated, swallowing hard.

"Practically all of them. I'm not trying to give you any false hope. If I wasn't so sure he'd be all right I wouldn't say so. But we've never had one lost kid from this area that we didn't eventually find."

"But he's not *in* this area now," my mother sobbed. "God knows where he could be by this time."

My father put his arms around her and held her.

Lieutenant Cohen stood up. "He might still be very close by," he told them. "Often they just get tired and settle down somewhere for a nap. He could be right in the neighborhood."

"Thank you, lieutenant," my father said absently. "I'm sure you're right."

"We'll keep in touch," he said. Jill and I walked him to the door.

He turned and looked at me appraisingly. "It's odd that you didn't predict this," he remarked. "Considering how psychic you are."

"She did!" Jill blurted out. "Weeks ago."

"Really? What did you do about it?"

"I didn't do anything," I said. "I didn't know what there was to do."

"I told her not to tell our parents," Jill said. "It would just have worried them and if it was going to happen there was nothing anyone could do to prevent it."

Somehow it didn't sound like such a convincing argument now that Dennis had actually disappeared. Lieutenant Cohen didn't seem to think so either. He gave us a very skeptical look before he spoke again.

"And isn't there anything you can do now?"

"What do you mean?"

"Well, if you're really psychic, why don't you go into a trance, or whatever it is you do, and find out where your brother is?"

"Laura!" Jill grabbed my arm. "That's a great idea! You could do it."

I looked anxiously from the lieutenant to my sister. "I don't know," I hesitated. "I've never tried anything like that before."

It would be wonderful if I could help find Dennis, but I was very uncertain about my ability to do it. All my predictions had seemed to be about

165

the future, and what Lieutenant Cohen was suggesting was that I psychically tune in on what was happening in the present. Like mind reading, I guess; get into Dennis's head and see where he was."

"I don't know. . . ."

"You can try," urged Jill.

"If it was my brother," Lieutenant Cohen said, "I'd certainly want to at least try."

I searched his face carefully for some clue to his real feelings. Was he daring me to find Dennis because he thought I was a fake and would give myself away if I couldn't do it? Or did he actually believe I was psychic and that maybe I really could help?

"I can't promise anything," I said at last.

"I know, Laura," Jill nodded. "We're just asking you to try."

"And I'm a little out of practice," I warned. "I haven't been doing it much lately."

"It's true," she agreed. "You really haven't had the time."

"But I'll try."

"I'll wait here," said Lieutenant Cohen, "so in case you come up with anything I can have it checked out right away."

I studied him again. I just couldn't figure out whether this was a challenge, or he sincerely hoped that I could find Dennis. His face was bland, revealing nothing.

"I'll go upstairs and see what I can do."

He nodded and sat down on the oak bench near the front door. He crossed his arms and leaned back, prepared to wait.

I went to my room and stretched out on the bed. At first I just tried to relax, like I had on the night of the play. I felt a great pressure, as if Dennis's safety depended on me.

And I was frightened of what I might find out.

But it had to be done. Since I did have the Gift, this might be my chance to use it for something really important, to do some good with it. To help.

I closed my eyes.

Dennis, I thought. Dennis. Where are you?

At first nothing happened. I just lay there, repeating his name over and over again. I opened my eyes a couple of times and saw that I was still in my room, still surrounded by the familiar things I saw every day.

But then . . . Crowds of people were milling around, carrying packages. At first, that was all I was aware of. But soon, as if picking him out of a crowd, I spotted Dennis. I seemed to be right behind him, following him as he went from place to place. But we didn't take much time getting places —he would appear in one spot, and then suddenly turn up somewhere else, while I found myself with him in one store after another.

He ate a big dish of ice cream. Then he was standing in front of a cage, looking at some puppies tumbling around on shredded newspaper. Then he was sitting in front of a huge color TV, watching cartoons. He rode a mechanical horse, feeding dimes into the slot again and again, while he bounced up and down on the painted saddle.

He went into someplace dark, where there was a big screen with moving images on it, and ate candy. Then he was walking up and down aisle after aisle of shelves filled with toys.

The moment I came out of it I knew exactly what I had seen.

I leaped off the bed and ran downstairs.

"The shopping mall," I said. "He's at the shopping mall, wandering around."

Lieutenant Cohen stretched his legs and stood up. "We thought of that already," he said. "We have the security people there alerted."

"But I'm sure that's where he is," I insisted. "I saw him."

My parents heard me. "You saw him?" my mother demanded. "When?"

"Just now—I got a psychic vision. He's at the mall, hacking around."

Jill ran to the closet and grabbed her coat.

"Let's go," she said.

"Oh, come now," Douglas scoffed. "You can't believe—"

"Wait a minute," urged Lieutenant Cohen, holding up his hands. "It's a big place. I'm sure he could spend hours without anyone spotting him. It's very possible—a lot of the kids go there. But don't run off all disorganized. Let's take this one step at a time."

He phoned the head of security at the shopping center. Douglas shot him a look of disgust, threw up his hands and went into the kitchen.

"His sister," Lieutenant Cohen was saying into the phone, "thinks he might be walking around the stores." He gave me a sideways glance. "Do you have enough people to check them in some kind of order? Well the department stores could page him again."

"Try the TV departments," I said. "If he's tired, he's probably sitting in front of a television set somewhere."

"Check the TV departments," he said, nodding in my direction. "He might have settled down there."

"The movies," I added. "He went to the movies. But I don't know if he's still there."

"And check out the movie too. Yeah, I know they're not supposed to, but he could have slipped in with a bunch of kids."

"I think we should go ourselves," said Jill. "We know what he looks like. And Laura knows where to look for him."

Lieutenant Cohen raised his eyebrows. "Well, it's a good logical guess," he admitted.

"It's not a guess! Laura *saw* him. Just because *you* couldn't find him—"

"Jill," my father interrupted, "take it easy. Now that they know where to look they can concentrate on that area."

"Look, Mr. Hoffman, I don't *know* anything,"

the lieutenant objected. "But as long as they've got the manpower over there to put in a good search we might as well try it. A lot of kids do turn up at the shopping center and it's a place where they can kill a lot of time without anyone noticing them. Whether or not your daughter is really psychic I can't say. But I'm willing to give her idea a try, if only to convince you that we're not going to overlook any possibility in finding your boy."

He left, promising to call us as soon as he found out anything.

We went to wait in the living room.

"You're sure, Laura?" my mother asked. "You really saw him?"

"I really did, but the thing is, I don't know exactly when I was seeing him. I mean, I was trying to concentrate on where he was right now, but I don't know for sure that's what I saw."

"You mean, it could be some time in the future?" Jill asked.

"Yeah. It usually *is* the future that I see; at least, I think it is."

"Well then, that's all right," said Jill. "Because even if you did see him in the future, that means he's okay now. Otherwise—" She stopped and looked around anxiously. "I mean—at least we know he *has* a future—" She stopped again, realizing how awful that sounded.

"It's all right." My mother managed a little smile. "We know what you mean."

Douglas joined us in the living room. Another half hour dragged on. As the minutes ticked away so did my confidence. Shouldn't they have found him by now? With all those people on the lookout for him, if he was at the mall he should have been spotted by this time. What if I'd been wrong? What if something had happened to him, something that I didn't see? I'd reassured my family that he was fine—but what if he wasn't?

Douglas sat opposite me, his arms crossed over his chest. Every once in a while he scowled in my direction.

The phone rang.

We all made a mad dash for it. My mother snatched up the receiver first.

"Yes? Oh, thank God! Is he all right? Where —he was *what?*"

Jill and Douglas and my father and I jumped around the hallway like kangaroos running amok, hugging each other and yelling.

"We'll be right down to get him," she shouted into the phone. "All right, put him on. Dennis? Dennis, we've been frantic about you! Why did you go off like that? Look, never mind, just stay with the policeman. Yes, I'm sure he's a policeman. We'll come and get you. Just—well, if you want to. Yes, it's okay. No, he's *not* a stranger, he's a *policeman.* Yes, you *can,* Well, check his identification then. I'm telling you it's okay. Put him back on."

"He wants to come home in the patrol car," she

said to us. "With the siren. But he's not allowed to get in cars with strangers." She shook her head hopelessly. My father sank into a chair.

"Do you believe it?" he said. "Do you believe him? He's not allowed to get in cars with strangers." He put his hand to his forehead and just stayed that way for awhile. We couldn't tell whether he was laughing or crying.

My mother got off the phone at last, and grabbed me around the waist, hugging me fiercely. "You were right," she cried, spinning me around and kissing me wildly all over my face. "You were one hundred percent right, you—you psychic Einstein. He was fast asleep in front of the biggest color TV in Macy's."

"But what took them so long?" I gasped, hugging her back.

"My description," she said wryly. "It never occurred to me that he might have dressed up before he left. The officer told me it would have been a lot easier to find him if we had told them he was wearing his pith helmet. They must have passed him fifty times, but they knew it couldn't be the kid they were looking for, because surely they would have been told right off the bat if they were supposed to watch for a kid in a pith helmet."

"How many people, after all," my father agreed weakly, "wear their pith helmets in February?"

"And his Mets jacket," my mother added. "In this weather! I hope he doesn't catch pneumonia.

Well, they had a completely wrong description of him. No wonder they couldn't find him."

"Funny," I mused. "I didn't see the pith helmet."

"How about it, Douglas?" Jill demanded. "Is this proof enough for you? Laura found him, didn't she?"

"A good, logical guess," he retorted, "like the cop said."

"You're impossible!"

"She didn't, he reminded us, "see the pith helmet."

"I give up," Jill said in disgust. "Laura could predict the world would end tomorrow in an atomic war, and as we all went down in flames, you'd be saying, 'She was wrong, she was wrong, they weren't atom bombs, they were hydrogen bombs."

A few moments later we heard a siren. My mother opened the front door. "I hear it, but I dont' see it yet."

"This kid," Douglas remarked, "is getting some royal treatment for pulling a rotten trick."

"You're right," my mother said. She tried to look stern. "But I want to find out why he did it before I break his neck. Oh, will I be glad to see him!"

We saw the flashing light of the patrol car as it turned down Woodbine Way. Our neighbors started to appear in their windows and at their front doors. As the car pulled up in our driveway the siren died away like a record slowing down to a moan.

"Tell the neighbors he's all right, Douglas," my mother ordered, running out to the car. She snatched Dennis up in her arms and carried him into the house, leaving my father to thank the policeman who'd brought him.

"Dennis Jay Hoffman, we were so worried about you we nearly died!" She yanked his pith helmet off and examined his face for any signs of injury.

"And you must be freezing in that light jacket! What in the world got into you?"

"Nothing," said Dennis. He snuggled comfortably against her neck.

"Nothing! Why did you go off on your own like that?"

"I finished counting to a million and there was nothing else to do."

"Congratulations," said my father.

"Thank you," replied Dennis.

"Why didn't you wait for me to take you to Roger's?"

"I did wait. I waited and waited, but you didn't get finished and the channel tuner broke so I went myself."

"But you didn't go to Roger's. You went to the shopping center."

"Yeah. I don't know how to go to Roger's."

My mother looked at my father in despair.

"At least he knows his own limitations," he ventured.

"Oh, *Basil!* Dennis, you are never, *never* to leave this house without telling me again! Do you understand me?"

"Okay. Did you hear me coming in the police car with the siren?"

"We heard you. The whole block heard you. Everyone was very worried about you, Dennis. You must *never* do that again."

"Okay. He put the flashing light on too. We went real fast. Right through red lights and everything."

"Are you hungry? You must be starved."

"No. I had ice cream and candy in the movies."

Douglas looked startled. He sat down heavily on the oak bench and frowned.

I smiled modestly.

"You're amazing," my father said, shaking his head. "Absolutely amazing."

"Thank you," said Dennis.

"I meant Laura," my father said sternly.

"Finally." I heaved a contented sigh.

My parents gave me a puzzled look. My mother put Dennis down and Jill took him off to the kitchen for some pizza—but not before giving Douglas a not-so-gentle poke in the chest.

I wanted the lovely moment to last. When they didn't say anything, I added, "I guess you're kind of proud of me now."

"Fishing for compliments?" Douglas inquired.

"Be quiet, Douglas," my father said. "What do you mean, 'finally'? What do you mean, 'proud of you now'?"

"Well, I mean, telling you where Dennis was—being psychic and all." It sounded silly, my having to say it myself. They were supposed to be telling *me* this.

"Oh, brother," said Douglas in disgust. He went upstairs, shaking his head.

"Laura," my father began hesitantly, "I think your ESP is amazing—like I said before. But why should it make us proud of you?"

"Because now I have a talent," I said. "Like Jill and Douglas. Now there's something I can do that you can be proud of me for." I felt like I was going to cry. After all this time, after everything that had happened, was I still just Laura? Plain old ordinary Laura?

I looked from one to the other of them desperately, waiting for them to tell me they thought I was special, wonderful, unique.

"But why should we be proud of something we had nothing to do with?" asked my mother. "*You're* the one who should be proud of *yourself.*"

"But you're proud of Jill and Douglas!" I *was* crying now. I couldn't help it. They wouldn't even *pretend* they were proud of me. Why couldn't they lie, or fake it or something, when they could see how much I wanted them to think I was special?

"Of course we're proud of them," my father

176

said. "Because they're our children and because they're turning out to be good people."

"I mean, because they're so talented," I insisted between sobs.

"Laura," my mother said, "I'm glad Douglas likes music and has found something he's good at. And I'm glad Jill likes to act and can do it well enough to get satisfaction from it. And I enjoy going to their concerts and plays and seeing them perform, because I know it makes them happy to be able to do these things. But that's not what makes them special to me. And your ESP isn't what makes *you* special to me. If Jill couldn't bowl at all, and Douglas wasn't captain of the debating team and you weren't psychic, I'd still think you were all wonderful—because you're my children. Even if no one else in the whole world thought you were special, *I* would."

I kept my head down. All I could do was let the tears come. My mother went off to the bathroom and came back with a box of tissues.

"Laura," my father began. "Laura, listen. It's not because of us that Douglas can play the piano. It was something in *him*. We had nothing to do with it, except that when we saw he seemed to be interested in music, we made piano lessons available to him. When Jill said she wanted to go bowling, we took her bowling. When she began to be interested in acting, she went and tried out for school plays and the drama club. But they discovered their own interests and abilities, and they developed them. They're the ones who should take pride in what they can do."

My mother handed me a bunch of tissues.

"It's not what you can do that makes us proud of you," she said. "It's what you *are*. Do you think I'd be proud of a son who composed a symphony at the age of three but who liked to pull wings off flies in his spare time?"

I giggled and shuddered at the same time.

"Do you see what I mean?"

I shook my head. "Not really."

"All right. Let's make it more personal. Let's take *you*. Which do you think would make us happier—if you were—oh, a mathematical genius, but spent your entire childhood bullying other children, or if you were a happy, well-adjusted kid who brightened up any room you walked into?"

"Why couldn't I be a well-adjusted mathematical genius?" I sniffled.

When she didn't answer, I looked up from my clump of wet tissues. Her forehead was furrowed in thought. My father was grinning.

"She has a very logical mind, Maggie," he said. "Why couldn't she be both?"

"Because this is *my* train of thought," my mother retorted, "and you're going to let me express it the way I want to."

"Train of thought," said Douglas, loping down the stairs. *"Express* it. Express train." He headed for the kitchen. "Very good, Mom," he called back.

She shook her head impatiently.

"The point is that I love my children because they're lovable, not because they can *do* things. The qualities that make you lovable have nothing to do with talent or genius. Why do you think your father loves me?" she asked suddenly.

"I—I don't know," I stammered. I thought about it for a moment. "Because you're *you*, I guess. That sounds stupid," I muttered.

"No it doesn't! Do you think he would love me less if I didn't write books? Do you think he would love me less if I hadn't been in the movies?"

"Of course not."

"Exactly! He doesn't love me for what I can do, or what I can produce—that's unimportant to him. He loves me for what I *am. Me.*"

Douglas passed by again with a slice of pizza in each hand.

"But your cooking helps," he commented.

"Scram, Douglas," she growled.

He took the stairs two at a time. "Just passing through."

"Do you see?"

"I guess so." I sighed. The tears had stopped. "You're saying you love me even though I'm not talented. It's just—well, maybe you don't realize it, but it's hard to be the only person in the whole family that nobody *admires*. That's why I was hoping you'd be proud of me when I found out I was psychic. Then you wouldn't just say, 'And this is Laura.'"

179

"What?" my father asked.

"Never mind. It's only—everybody in this whole family is exceptional except me. I mean, before I was psychic there wasn't one thing that made me outstanding. And Jill and Douglas—and you—" I said, almost accusingly to my mother, "actually have two things. It's not fair." Even to me, that sounded childish. I started to cry again.

"If you insist on judging yourself that way," my father said, "even though you know how unimportant it is to us, you have two things now too. You're psychic and you can act. And as you get older you'll find more things that you're good at. Your mother didn't start to write books until she was thirty. Nobody knew when she was twelve that she was a budding author. Jill and Douglas are both older than you are. They've had more time to discover what their abilities are."

"Maybe Laura's problem," my mother suggested, "is that she's good at too many things."

"What?" I was surprised out of my crying. I examined her face to see if she was putting me on.

"Well, dear, even you have to admit you get practically straight A's in everything."

"Oh, *school*."

"If you only got A's in English, for instance," she went on calmly, "then you'd figure English was your best subject. Even if you flunked everything else, you'd know you were really good at English. But since you get A's in everything, somehow

180

you've decided that means you're good at nothing."

"That's ridiculous," I grumbled.

"I agree with you," she said.

"The whole point is," my father said firmly, "that we are proud of you because of the fine person you're turning out to be and you're not finished yet, so there's no way for you or anyone else to know what you're going to be able to do in the future."

"You forget," Jill said, carrying a drowsy Dennis past us, "that you're talking to a psychic. Couldn't help overhearing," she added. "Why don't you look into your future, Laura? You gave readings for everyone but yourself. Typical, isn't it?" She grunted, staggering up the stairs under Dennis's weight. "She's so selfish and greedy and spoiled, that's why we all can't stand her." Her voice trailed away as she disappeared into Dennis's room.

I couldn't help smiling. At least I knew Jill appreciated me.

"Are you feeling a little better now?" asked my father.

"A little." Actually I didn't feel a great deal better, but I was tired from all that crying. And I didn't think there was anything more they could say that would change the way I'd felt for so long.

"I think I'll go up and lie down awhile."

I trudged up the stairs and sank down on my bed. I really was exhausted. But Jill's idea appealed to me. Why not look into my own future? Maybe I'd see something there which would change the whole way I felt about myself.

I closed my eyes.

I was looking at a playbill. At the top was printed: "LAURA: A PLAY IN THREE ACTS."

I seemed to be in a darkened theater. I looked down at the program again, and read, "ACT I: LAURA IS BORN. The curtain rose and my mother walked onstage, carrying a baby in her arms. She was talking softly to it, and cuddling it as she made her way across the stage. I couldn't hear any sounds, but she had her head close to the baby's and her lips moved. She turned to face the audience, and held the baby up for everyone to see. She took a deep bow, and walked off.

The curtain fell. I looked around at all the people in the theater and saw they were applauding. I still didn't hear any sounds.

The curtain rose. My program read, "ACT II: LAURA'S CHILDHOOD." A little girl—me, I guess—skipped across the stage, trailed by a very small boy who could barely toddle after her. He must have been Dennis. She sat down in the center of the stage and the boy plopped down next to her. From either side of the wings appeared Jill and Douglas. They walked to center stage and positioned themselves formally behind me and Dennis. My father and mother emerged from backstage and took their places behind the children. They all stayed immobile for a moment, as if posing for a stiff family photograph. Then the little girl and boy stood up and the whole group bowed toward the audience.

The curtain came down, and once again everyone applauded.

I waited eagerly for the curtain to rise once more. It was taking a long time. Yet no one around me seemed restless or impatient. They just sat, with bland smiles on their faces, quietly waiting. I was the only one in the theater who was in a hurry for the third act to begin.

Still nothing happened. The house lights didn't go up, but neither did the curtain. Puzzled, I squinted down at the program. It read, "ACT III: TO BE CONTINUED."

I felt terribly confused. I began to turn the program every which way, looking for some clue as to what was going to happen. But all the rest of the print on it was blurred, unreadable. Frantically I turned the paper over and over, until I suddenly noticed something written in little letters right underneath "TO BE CONTINUED." It was "By Laura. All in good time."

About the Author

Ellen Conford lives in Massapequa, New York, with her husband, her son, and assorted pets. Miss Conford believes that "children like to read about things that could never possibly happen to them, and they like to read about the kinds of things that happen to them all the time. I write about the latter." Miss Conford has also written *Dear Lovey Hart, I am Desperate, Me and the Terrible Two, The Luck of Pokey Bloom, Felicia the Critic,* and *The Alfred G. Graebner Memorial High School Handbook of Rules and Regulations* (a novel). The last four titles are available in Archway Paperback editions.

POCKET BOOKS

ARCHWAY
PAPERBACKS

Other titles you will enjoy

29545 A GIFT OF MAGIC, by Lois Duncan. Illustrated by Arvis Stewart. Nancy's talent for extrasensory perception stirs up tension and danger for her as she becomes aware of the true extent of her special powers. (75¢)

29717 THE HOUSE AT 12 ROSE STREET, by Mimi Brodsky. Illustrated by David Hodges. Bobby Myers has to come to grips with the problem of racial conflict after a black family moves into his all-white suburban community. (95¢)

29830 THE GHOST NEXT DOOR, by Wylly Folk St. John. Illustrated by Trina Schart Hyman. Strange signs of the existence of a ghost next door trigger the curiosity of Lindsey and Tammy, who resolve to find out just what's happening. ($1.25)

29726 THE HAPPY DOLPHINS, by Samuel Carter III. Illustrated with photographs. The author explores many intriguing facets of dolphin behavior as he tells the true story of Dal and Suwa, two bottle-nosed dolphins that made friends with humans. ($1.25)

29778 THE HOUSE OF THIRTY CATS, by Mary Calhoun. Illustrated by Mary Chalmers. Adventure and excitement enter Sarah's life when she pays her first visit to Miss Tabitha's wonderful house, meets the members of the cat community, and chooses a kitten of her very own. ($1.50)

29740 THE TRUE STORY OF OKEE THE OTTER, by Dorothy Wisbeski. Illustrated with photographs. The beloved pet of a suburban family, Okee is a happy-go-lucky clown, curious about everything, and in and out of mischief. ($1.25)

29809 ME AND THE TERRIBLE TWO, by Ellen Conford. Illustrated by Charles Carroll. When her best friend moves away, Dorrie is certain that she'll never be happy again—especially with those two impossible twin boys who move in next door. ($1.25)

29509 ALVIN FERNALD, MAYOR FOR A DAY, by Clifford B. Hicks. Illustrated by Bill Sokol. During his one-day administration, Alvin tackles the problems of Riverton and gets unexpected, hilarious results. (75¢)

(If your bookseller does not have the titles you want, you may order them by sending the retail price, plus 35¢ for postage and handling, to: Mail Service Department, POCKET BOOKS, a Simon & Schuster Division of Gulf & Western Corporation, 1230 Avenue of the Americas, New York, N. Y. 10020. Please enclose check or money order—do not send cash.)